LOVE FINDS A HOME

LOVE
FINDS A
HOME

JANETTE OKE

BETHANY HOUSE PUBLISHERS
MINNEAPOLIS, MINNESOTA 55438
A Division of Bethany Fellowship, Inc.

oke

1261

Cover illustration by Dan Thornberg,
Bethany House Publishers staff artist.

Published by Bethany House Publishers
A Division of Bethany Fellowship, Inc.
6820 Auto Club Road, Minneapolis, Minnesota 55438

Printed in the United States of America

Library of Congress Cataloging-in-Publication Data

Oke, Janette, 1935–
    Love finds a home / Janette Oke.
        p.   cm. — (Love comes softly ; 8)
    Sequel to: Love takes wing.

    I. Title. II. Series: Oke, Janette, 1935–
Love comes softly series ; 8.
PR9199.3.038L56   1989
813'.54—dc20   89–32731
ISBN 1-55661-086-6   CIP

To Ingolf Arnesen my Christian brother,
prayer partner, and cheering section—
friend of the Davises, Joneses and Delaneys.
Thank you for your friendship, support and prayers.
God bless!

Table of Contents

Some of the Characters in the LOVE COMES SOFTLY Series

Clark and Marty Davis—partners in a marriage in which each had lost a previous spouse.

Missie—Clark's daughter from his first marriage, married Willie LaHaye and moved west to ranch.

Clare—Marty's son born after her first husband's death, married Kate. They lived in the same farmyard as Clark and Marty. Their children—Amy Jo, Dan, David and Dack.

Arnie—Clark and Marty's first child. He married Anne and had three sons—Silas, John and Abe.

Daughter Ellie—married Lane Howard and moved west to join Missie and Willie. Their children were Brenda, William and Willis.

Son Luke—trained to be a doctor and returned to the small town to practice medicine. He married Abbie. Their children were Thomas, Aaron, and Ruth.

Jackson Brown—the schoolfriend who greatly impressed Melissa, Amy Jo and Belinda when he first arrived at the country school.

Belinda—Clark and Marty's youngest daughter who trained as a nurse and went to Boston.

Chapter 1

Stirrings

Belinda opened her eyes slightly against the glare of the morning sun, then quickly closed them and pulled the blanket up around her face for protection. It was early—too early to rise—but she wouldn't be able to sleep with the sun shining in her eyes.

Even in her sleepy state she knew something was unusual. Other mornings she had not awakened with the sun shining directly in her window. "The drapes—where are the drapes?" she wondered groggily. And then things began to filter back into her foggy consciousness.

It was the moon that had kept her from pulling the drapes the night before. *It's so full and golden and shining,* she had commented to herself when she went to shut it out. She impulsively decided to watch it as she lay in her bed. She would get up later, she thought, when the moon had passed from view and properly close the heavy curtains.

But sleep had claimed her before the moon moved out of sight, and now the sun was streaming in her window, refusing to allow her further sleep.

Belinda pulled back her covers and crawled from bed. If she was to get any more sleep, she had to shut out the early morning sunshine. Still tired, she yawned as she reached for the pull, but she couldn't resist looking out at the bright summer day.

Already the elderly gardener, Thomas, was bending over the

13

flower beds, coaxing begonias to lift their bright summer faces to the sun. *What beautiful flower beds he's laid out,* Belinda thought. *Why, Aunt Virgie said just yesterday that she doesn't know what in the world she will do should Thomas decide to retire.*

Belinda smiled affectionately as she watched the old gardener. She did not share her employer's fears. She could see his love for the flowers in his every careful move. One might as well ask Thomas to stop breathing as to stop nursing his beloved flower beds.

Sudden determination made Belinda drop the drapery pull. With such a beautiful day beckoning her, she could no longer stay in bed. She would dress and slip out to join Thomas. Maybe he would even let her pull a few weeds.

Belinda hummed as she slipped a simple gown over her head and tied a bow at her waist. Aunt Virgie would not waken for some time yet, and Belinda would be free to enjoy the early morning hours.

She carried her walking shoes in her hand so she would not make any noise. Leaving her door slightly ajar so as not to disturb her employer, she slipped silently from the room and descended the steps.

Belinda left the house by the veranda door, and paused on the steps to breathe deeply. The heavy scent and beauty of summer blossoms filled her senses. *It truly is beautiful at Marshall Manor,* Belinda decided for the umpteenth time. Her longing to be back in her small-town prairie setting was not because she did not appreciate her present surroundings. Her people, her family, were the reason her yearning thoughts so often turned toward home. And thinking of them, as lately she seemed to do almost constantly, her heart ached for a chance to be a part of their lives again.

But Belinda refused to dwell on her loneliness. As she had often done in the past, she firmly pushed it aside and thought instead of the things she had to be thankful for.

Mrs. Stafford-Smyth had been sick for almost two weeks with a serious bout of flu, but now, thankfully, she seemed to be gaining strength each day. Belinda breathed a sigh of relief.

It wasn't the constant nursing or the loss of sleep at nights that bothered Belinda. It was the worry—the possibility that her friend might not be able to shake the illness.

Belinda loved the elderly woman almost as though she were truly kin. They even enjoyed their own little game of "belonging" to one another. Mrs. Stafford-Smyth had asked Belinda if she minded calling her Aunt Virgie, and Belinda had been pleased to comply. In turn, "Aunt Virgie" always referred to Belinda as "Belinda, deah," with her intriguing eastern accent. The arrangement satisfied them both.

The lady seemed to have long ago concluded that neither grandson—Pierre, and his Anne-Marie, nor Franz, and his Yvette—would ever consent to share her Boston home with her. Indeed, Pierre and Anne-Marie had sent word from France that they were soon to be joined by a third family member. Aunt Virgie and Belinda, both rejoicing over the great-grandchild to come, had even sat and knitted gifts to go to the new baby. But both had decided silently it was most unlikely that Mrs. Stafford-Smyth would ever personally see or hold the child.

Belinda stopped to admire a climbing rose. The bright pink bloom filled the morning air with a sweet sunshine all its own. Mrs. Stafford-Smyth said that Thomas had developed the lovely flower in his own greenhouse. Belinda breathed deeply of its scent, then moved on into the garden.

McIntyre, Thomas's companion of many years, slipped alongside to sniff at Belinda's hand.

"Good morning, Mac," Belinda greeted him, running a hand over his graying head. "I see you're up early, too." The old dog's eyesight was failing and his hearing was not as sharp as it had been, but he never missed an opportunity to be at his master's side.

Thomas heard the words and straightened slowly, blinking as though not sure he was seeing right. He put one hand to his creaking back, then grinned slowly, showing a few gaps where teeth were missing.

"Miss Belinda," he said, "how come ye not be abed?"

"It's too nice a morning to sleep," Belinda answered good-naturedly.

But Thomas responded with a twinkle in his eyes, " 'Tis jest the same as any other mornin', 'tis."

Belinda smiled. "I suppose so," she admitted slowly. "I really wouldn't know. But once I saw the day, I couldn't resist getting out into it. It will be hot and stuffy later on, I'm thinking." And Belinda cast a glance at the bright sky with the sun already streaming down rays of warmth.

"Aye," spoke Thomas. " 'Twill be a hot one today, I'm afraid."

"I noticed your rosebush is covered with flowers," Belinda went on. "It smells most wonderful."

Thomas grinned widely at her comment. "Aye" was all he said.

He bent back to his work again, and Belinda ventured closer and knelt down beside him.

"Could I—would you mind if—if I pulled a few weeds?" she asked timidly.

"Weedin' ye wish?" His eyes widened at the thought of milk-white hands in such an endeavor. "Ye pulled weeds afore?"

"Oh yes," quickly responded Belinda. "Back home I always helped with the garden."

"Ye had ye flowers?"

"Oh, not like here," Belinda was quick to explain. "Nothing nearly as grand as this. But Mama's always had her flowers. Roses and violets and early spring tulips. She loves flowers, Mama does. But she spends most of her time in the big garden— vegetables, grown for family use. Mama has fed her family almost all year round from the fruits of her garden." Belinda's voice had grown nostalgic just thinking about it. She could see Marty's form bent over the hoe or lifting hot canning jars from the steaming kettle.

"Aye," said old Thomas, nodding his head in understanding. "My mither, she did too." Belinda thought his eyes looked a little misty.

"Be at it, then," Thomas gave her permission. "Mind ye pick careful. An' don't prick a finger on a thorn." Then Thomas handed her his own little hand trowel, and Belinda leaned forward and let her fingers feel the warmth of the sun-heated soil.

They worked in silence side by side for some time before Thomas spoke again. " 'Tis a new rose, I have now. In the greenhouse. It has its first blossom just about to open. Ye wish to see it?"

Belinda straightened her arched back, eyes glistening. "Oh, could I?" she asked eagerly.

"Aye," the old man said with a slight nod. He lifted himself slowly to his feet, easing the ache from his slightly hunched shoulders. Then he cast his eyes around the yard to find old Mac. The gardener never took a step without checking on his dog. With Mac's senses no longer what they had been, he feared the dog might not detect his departure.

"McIntyre," he spoke loudly now, "we be movin' on."

Belinda loved to hear him speak the dog's name. He rolled the "r" off his tongue so effectively.

The dog lifted his head, then slowly pulled himself to his feet. He moved to Thomas's side and as one they moved toward the greenhouse.

Belinda fell into step beside them. She stopped only once—by the side of the climbing rose.

"It's so pretty," she murmured, touching a leaf gently.

"Aye," acknowledged old Thomas with a twinkle and he reached out a hand and stroked a velvety petal. " 'Tis Pink Rosanna, I call 'er."

"You gave it a name?" asked Belinda in surprise.

"Aye. I always name my new ladies." Belinda smiled at his description of his new rose hybrids.

They walked on to the greenhouse, and Belinda waited while old Thomas carefully opened the creaking door. McIntyre found his own gunny sack by the entrance and flopped down. Even Old McIntyre was not allowed further admittance into Thomas's sanctuary.

Belinda followed slowly, wanting to exclaim over and over as her eyes swept the massive foliage and glorious blooms, but she held her tongue.

At last they were standing before a small rose bush. With obvious skill and affection, it had been grafted onto another shoot. Belinda could see the slight enlargement where the grafting had taken place. But her eye passed swiftly from the stem to the delicate bud that was just beginning to unfurl. On the same stem, another bud had formed, and a third one was slowly breaking from curled greenery.

"Oh," murmured Belinda, unable to restrain herself. "It's—it's so beautiful. I've never seen such a pretty rose—such a combination of lovely colors."

Thomas could not repress his smile or the shine in his eyes. "Aye," he nodded, and his gnarled old hand reached forward to caress the flower.

Then, before Belinda could catch her breath, he lifted his sharp pruning scissors and snipped the flower from the stem and extended it to her.

Belinda reached out her hand and then just as quickly withdrew it. "But—but—" she stammered.

"Go on wit' ye now," the old gardener said, easing the bloom into her hand. " 'Tis only fitting ye be the one to have the first bloom." He lowered his eyes to his worn-out gardener's shoes. When he lifted them again, Belinda detected a flush on his weathered cheeks. "I named her Belinda," he confessed. "Princess Belinda."

For a long moment Belinda could say nothing. Her hand slowly curled around the flower and she raised it to her face. Breathing deeply of the fragrance, she brushed her lips against the soft petals. She felt her eyes filling with unbidden tears. "It's beautiful," she whispered. "Thank you, Thomas."

"Aye," the old man nodded. " 'Tis my thanks to ye fer bein' so kind to M'lady."

Belinda understood his simple explanation. She nodded in return, then smiled and carefully found her way outside.

As she walked back toward the veranda, Belinda studied the flower in her hands. The soft cream of each petal slowly blended into a deeper yellow, which in turn changed into an apricot. Belinda was sure she had never seen such a pretty rose. *To think Thomas named it after me!* she marveled. She felt at once exalted and deeply humbled.

Belinda lifted her face to the sun, now higher in the eastern sky. The summer day was well on its way. Aunt Virgie would soon be awakening. Belinda knew she must hurry to bathe and change from her soiled gardening gown. No longer tired, there was a spring to her step and a light in her eyes. She was ready to face this new day. She smiled to herself.

Her eyes fell back to the exquisite rose.

What a difference one bright flower can make in a person's life, she mused. But then she corrected herself. *No,* she reasoned, *it isn't the flower—pretty as it is. It is a person who has brought joy to my heart. Thomas. A dear old man—just a gardener in some folks' thinking—but a beautiful person. One I have learned to love.*

The thought did not surprise Belinda. There were many older people in the household whom she had learned to love. Aunt Virgie, old Thomas, the straight-laced Windsor, Cook— even the stern-faced Potter. Belinda smiled to herself. She loved them all, actually. They were part of her life. Her Boston family.

Oh, she knew other people her own age pitied her, being "stuck in a houseful of the elderly," but Belinda didn't feel shut in, restless and forgotten. Not since she had given God the proper recognition in her life. She felt loved and protected— and needed. *If only—if only I didn't feel so lonesome for those back home, I could be quite satisfied and fulfilled living and working at Marshall Manor,* she recognized.

Chapter 2

Aunt Virgie

"Good morning, Aunt Virgie," Belinda said softly, proceeding into the room when she had determined that Mrs. Stafford-Smyth was awake.

The frail woman managed a smile. "Mawnin', Belinda, deah," she answered.

"Did you sleep?" asked Belinda as she went to open the drapes, knowing that it was some time since the older woman had enjoyed a good night's rest.

"I did. Scarce can believe it myself, but I did. Oh, and it felt—delicious, too," she said with emphasis. "But you know what? I feel that now I remembah *how* to sleep—I could just sleep on and on."

"Then perhaps you should. You haven't slept decently for days—or rather nights," Belinda corrected herself with a grin.

Mrs. Stafford-Smyth smiled weakly at Belinda's little joke. "You need sleep every bit as much as I," she informed Belinda. "You've been up night aftah night. I declayah, I don't know how you do it."

Belinda leaned over the bed and laid a hand on the silvery head. "I'm fine," she smiled. "In fact, I feel just great this morning. I've even been out weeding with Thomas."

Mrs. Stafford-Smyth showed her surprise. "You have—at this hou-ah?"

Belinda nodded. "And you should just see the new rose

21

bush!" she exclaimed, "It's covered with the most exquisite roses. And they smell just wonderful."

Belinda thought of her other bit of news. She hardly knew how to tell it so it wouldn't sound boastful, yet she had to share her delight with the older woman.

"And something else, too," she said, her eyes shining. "Thomas took me to his greenhouse."

The building was always referred to as "Thomas's greenhouse," and no one else would have dreamed of trespassing. The truth was, the greenhouse, like every other building on the grounds, belonged to Mrs. Stafford-Smyth.

"He did?" said Mrs. Stafford-Smyth, duly impressed.

"He did—and more than that. He showed me a brand-new rose that he has developed. He hasn't even set it outside in the gardens yet. It had its first flower—though others are coming quickly."

"I declayah!" said Mrs. Stafford-Smyth, enjoying the telling of the tale as much as the story itself. It had been some time since she had seen Belinda so elated, so alive.

"You will never guess what he has named the new rose," Belinda continued, then paused.

"Aftah some lovely lady, I suppose," mused Mrs. Stafford-Smyth. "They always do, it seems."

Belinda blushed.

"Well, I hardly expect he named it Old Prune Face, aftah me," teased the elderly lady.

"Oh, Aunt Virgie," protested Belinda, "no one would ever say that about you."

Mrs. Stafford-Smyth just smiled. "Well, they should," she said matter-of-factly. "I declayah, I looked in my hand mirrah befoah I went to bed last night, and I've lost some more weight. I do look like a prune, foah sure."

She has lost weight, Belinda acknowledged silently as she looked at the haggard face.

"Well, now that you are able to eat again," Belinda assured the lady, "Cook'll have you fattened up in no time." She smiled as she fluffed up a pillow and made the woman more comfortable.

"But you were telling me about that new rose," encouraged Mrs. Stafford-Smyth. "What did Thomas name it?"

"Let me show you the rose," said Belinda quickly.

"You mean, he picked one—already? He nevah does that."

"Well, he picked this one—the very first blossom," beamed Belinda. "Let me run get it. I have it in a bud vase in my room."

"I declayah!" exclaimed the woman.

Belinda soon returned with her cherished flower.

"Oh, my," Mrs. Stafford-Smyth said, her voice properly respectful, "it is a lovely one, isn't it? I hope he chose an equally pretty name."

Belinda felt her face flushing again. "Well, he—" she began. "He—honored me by naming the rose Belinda." Her face flaming, she wished she had never shared her secret. Mrs. Stafford-Smyth would think her dreadfully uppity.

But the older lady beamed. "How very apt," she smiled her appreciation. "Thomas is an astute old gentleman. He named a beautiful rose aftah a beautiful lady."

Belinda blushed further as she accepted the compliment.

"*Just* Belinda?" asked the woman further. "Often Thomas has added a descriptive word—something else to go with the lady's name."

"Princess Belinda," admitted Belinda, lowering her face to hide her embarrassment.

"Princess Belinda—that is nice. That's quite an honah, you know, to have one feel so about you," said the elderly lady.

Belinda was able to face her then.

"It really wasn't me he honored," she explained. "The name shows his feeling about you. You see, he named the flower after me because"—Belinda struggled to find the appropriate words—"because he wished—he wished to express his appreciation to me for—for caring for you. You are the one who is special to him."

Mrs. Stafford-Smyth stared wide-eyed at Belinda.

"Me? Why, whatevah do you mean? What did he say?" she probed.

"He said something like *for carin' for M'lady,*" Belinda said evenly.

"How sweet," murmured Mrs. Stafford-Smyth, blinking against tears forming in her eyes. She was silent for several minutes as Belinda busied herself about the room. Finally she spoke again, softly. "You know, one gets to thinking sometimes that one is really no worth at all. Life could just go right on without you and no one would scarcely notice." She sighed, then went on. "Heah I lie day aftah day, no good to anyone. And then—then a deah old friend, a gardenah, shows you he cares. Makes one wish to get bettah again."

"Oh, Aunt Virgie," Belinda cried, moving swiftly to the side of the elderly woman and touching her cheek gently. "The whole household has been tiptoeing about, hardly daring to breathe. We've all been worried half sick that you might—might not get better. We all need you—love you. Do you really have any doubt about that?"

The lady stirred almost restlessly and smiled back at Belinda.

"I'm a foolish old woman," she answered softly. "I have so much to live for, so many deah friends. I don't deserve them, but I'm so thankful for them." She sighed again and stirred in her bed, shoving a pillow away with a pale hand.

"Belinda, deah," she said with determination, "bring me my robe and slippahs."

At Belinda's little gasp of mild protest, Mrs. Stafford-Smyth hurried on, saying, "One nevah gains strength by lying abed. I've got a lot of convalescing to do if I want to enjoy this summah before it's gone. I'd best get at it. The blue robe, please."

Belinda did not argue further. Once Mrs. Stafford-Smyth had made up her mind, it was useless to argue with her.

Belinda went for the blue robe, glad that the woman had requested the warmest robe in her closet.

Lifting the garment from the hook, Belinda felt an enormous weight fall from her shoulders. It had been some time since she had seen such a sparkle in her employer's eyes. Truly she was on the road to recovery. Belinda could hardly wait to rush out to the kitchen to share the news with the rest of the household. They all had been worried.

"The first thing you need is a good breakfast," she stated as she helped the older woman into the robe and slippers. Belinda was about to ring for Windsor when there was a light tapping on the door. Belinda opened it on silent hinges. She could see the concern in Windsor's eyes. "Is M'lady awake?" he asked in a raspy whisper.

"Yes. Yes," Belinda assured him. "Come in. She's much better this morning. In fact, I was about to ring to have a breakfast tray prepared."

Windsor could not hide his relief, as practiced as he was in concealing his emotions.

"Come in, Windsah," called Mrs. Stafford-Smyth.

He stepped cautiously into the room, his hands fidgeting nervously. "Thomas wished to know if you'd like a bouquet, madam," he announced with proper dignity.

"Oh, yes," agreed Mrs. Stafford-Smyth, a smile lifting the weariness from her face.

Windsor turned on his heels with a sharp click. "I shall be right back, M'lady," he assured her and left the room.

While Windsor was gone Belinda hurried about, helping Mrs. Stafford-Smyth with her grooming and settling her in the comfortable chair by the open window.

Sarah came with two trays of nourishing food. For the first time in weeks, Mrs. Stafford-Smyth looked with some interest at the meal. Belinda smiled with relief and set a tray in front of the woman, accepting the other tray of food for herself.

They had just said grace together when there was another tap on the door. Windsor was back again with a bowl of fragrant, freshly cut pink roses. Belinda recognized them immediately.

"That's the new climbing rose bush on the back walk," she commented. "The one I told you about earlier. That's Thomas's new Pink Rosanna."

"Pink Rosanna," mused Mrs. Stafford-Smyth. "What a lovely name." She buried her face in the bowl of flowers. "And what beautiful flowers," she added.

Mrs. Stafford-Smyth stroked a soft petal, then breathed again the sweet smell of the flowers.

"Tell Thomas thank you for the flowers," she said, her voice husky. "I—I am deeply, deeply appreciative."

Windsor nodded and departed as Mrs. Stafford-Smyth lifted her head and smiled.

Belinda took the rose bowl gently and set it on the small table close beside the woman.

"We'd best eat our breakfast before it gets cold," she said softly and Mrs. Stafford-Smyth nodded in agreement.

From then on, Belinda noted that Mrs. Stafford-Smyth grew a bit stronger each day. It wasn't long before she was able to be up and about for short periods of time, and then she could walk the upstairs halls. At last she was able to make her way down to the rooms below. She enjoyed the summer sunshine as she sat with her needlework in the north parlor. She spent hours out on the veranda absorbing the smell and beauty of the garden. She presided once again over meals in the dining room. Belinda felt they had all been given a new lease on life. The whole household took on a new atmosphere—of thanksgiving and relief.

Belinda was thankful that she could once again leave the house occasionally. She had especially missed the Sunday services at church. She was so glad to drink deeply from the stirring hymns, the Sunday scriptures, and, yes, even the pastor's message. She could hardly wait for the time when Mrs. Stafford-Smyth would be able to rejoin her in the worship. *But I mustn't rush her,* Belinda reminded herself. *She has been very ill. It wouldn't do for her to have a relapse.*

Belinda decided that she would be patient. But, oh, it was so good to feel the burden of worry slip away from her, from the house and its staff. The summer days seemed brighter, the flowers fairer, the food tastier—everything seemed better to Belinda now that Mrs. Stafford-Smyth was well again.

Chapter 3

Plans

As the summer progressed, Mrs. Stafford-Smyth again took over the running of Marshall Manor, giving her daily orders to Windsor, Potter and Cook. Belinda was able to catch up on her sleep, her mending, her letter-writing and her shopping. She gave a relieved sigh every time she thought of the trying weeks of early summer. She hadn't realized just how deeply she had worried, how frightened she had been, how wearing were the weeks when Mrs. Stafford-Smyth had needed her constant care.

Each morning she met Mrs. Stafford-Smyth in the well-lit north parlor where they breakfasted together and planned their day. Then Belinda read a scripture portion and led them in a daily prayer. Belinda kept hoping for the day when Mrs. Stafford-Smyth would want to pray aloud too.

Mrs. Stafford-Smyth did attend church services regularly and gave the staff Sunday morning off so that they might do likewise. And though lately she seemed more interested in things of faith, yet she never expressed to Belinda her true thoughts on the matter.

Belinda longed to have someone she could discuss spiritual things with, but the senior pastor of the local congregation was much too busy to be bothered by a young woman who just wanted to talk. The associate pastor was a single man, not much older than Belinda herself. Though Belinda knew she could enjoy discussing issues of faith with a seminary graduate,

27

she also knew better than to suggest such a thing. Everyone, including the young minister himself, would surely think Belinda had no other intention than to snare an eligible young man. Belinda had no desire to open herself up to such gossip.

So Belinda continued on each day, enjoying the time spent in Bible reading and prayer but longing for spiritual fellowship. *If only—if only Aunt Virgie could understand and share my feelings,* she kept thinking.

But another thought concerned her. *If Aunt Virgie were to die now, would she be ready for heaven?* The idea troubled Belinda. She loved the woman dearly, and the thought of her not being prepared for death made Belinda spend even more time in prayer for her friend.

Toward the end of summer Mrs. Stafford-Smyth decided to host another dinner party. Belinda by now was used to socializing with her employer's wealthy and influential friends. She didn't dread the prospect of another such dinner as Pierre had done during his last visit to the household. *In fact,* Belinda conceded, *it is much better to have elderly company than no company at all.* She and Aunt Virgie needed some kind of diversion.

"What should we serve for dinnah, deah?" asked Mrs. Stafford-Smyth as they sat together in the downstairs parlor.

Belinda looked up from her needlepoint. She really cared little what was served for dinner, but she thought that would be an inappropriate response.

Instead she said mildly, "Perhaps Cook would have some suggestions."

Mrs. Stafford-Smyth considered that possibility. "Yes," she agreed at length. "I'm sure she would—but since this is my first dinnah party in such a long time, I'd rathah like to plan it myself."

Belinda smiled. "If you'd like to, then by all means you must."

"I was thinking of roast beef and Yorkshire pudding," went on the woman. "With asparagus tips and spiced carrots."

"That sounds good," agreed Belinda.

"We'll have a vegetable salad, with Cook's special dressing."

"And her poppy-seed rolls," suggested Belinda.

Mrs. Stafford-Smyth smiled. She had coaxed Belinda into sharing the planning.

"What about dessert?" asked the older woman.

"Oh, my," said Belinda with a sigh. "I shouldn't even *think* about dessert. I'm sure I've put on some pounds the last few weeks."

"And well you needed to," Mrs. Stafford-Smyth stated firmly. "You spoke of fattening me up. I declayah, you must have lost about as much weight during my flu bout as I did."

Belinda was sure it hadn't been all that much. She wanted to protest but let the matter drop.

"Cheesecake would be nice," Mrs. Stafford-Smyth mused aloud.

"Or fresh strawberry shortcake," responded Belinda.

"Does Thomas still have strawberries?"

"He says he has a second crop," answered Belinda. "He is really proud of them."

"Fresh strawberry shortcake it will be then. I nevah tire of strawberries, and we might as well enjoy them as long as they last," reasoned Mrs. Stafford-Smyth. "Ring for Cook, deah," she said to Belinda's nod. "I'd like to get this settled now."

Cook arrived with a fresh apron neatly covering her plump form. A bit anxious as she often was when being summoned to the sitting room, her face soon relaxed as her employer began to talk of dinner plans.

"And Miss Belinda would like some of your tasty poppy-seed rolls," Mrs. Stafford-Smyth went on, bringing a smile to Cook's face. "And for dessert, I understand Thomas has another crop of strawberries. We'll have your strawberry shortcake. Everyone loves that."

Cook openly beamed in spite of herself. She loved compliments on her cuisine—especially when the recognition came from her employer.

"We will serve dinnah at seven," went on Mrs. Stafford-Smyth.

Belinda smiled. She knew that Mrs. Celia Prescott would

be invited and, as Pierre had remarked so long ago, "Aunt Celia's never on time."

But on the night of the first dinner party in ages at Marshall Manor, Celia Prescott was *almost* on time. She breathlessly fluttered in and greeted her hostess. "Virgie, deah, I am *so* glad that you are up and about again! I was worried to *death* about you. You had that dreadful old flu for such a long, long time, I feahed that you'd *nevah* recovah!"

"I'm fine now," Mrs. Stafford-Smyth assured her calmly. "I've had good care." And she cast an appreciative glance toward Belinda.

"I have long since admired your foresight in having your own personal nurse," commented Mrs. Prescott with a hint of envy. "I don't know how you'd evah manage without her."

"Nor I," agreed Mrs. Stafford-Smyth with feeling.

Belinda flushed uncomfortably, which seemed to please Mrs. Allenby, one of the other guests. Belinda still could not warm to the woman. She seemed to take great pleasure in the discomfort of others. Thankfully, all the guests were now present, and they were able to move to the dining room where Windsor and Sarah were waiting to serve.

Chatting and laughing together, the evening passed sociably enough. Mrs. Celia Prescott humorously shared her adventures of the summer, to Mr. Walsh's great merriment. Mrs. Allenby gave an occasional imperious sniff as her contribution to the evening, while Mrs. Whitley smiled benignly on all. Her husband made up for her silence by firmly expressing himself on every subject. All in all, it was a lively evening, and Belinda reasoned that it was good for Mrs. Stafford-Smyth to have someone besides her to talk to.

But when the evening ended, Belinda felt a strange emptiness. A lonesomeness gnawed within her.

You just feel some sort of letdown after all the planning and anticipation are done, she scolded herself. *Aunt Virgie likely feels it, too.*

Belinda quickly slipped out of her crimson party gown and

into a cream-colored robe. She would help Mrs. Stafford-Smyth prepare for bed.

If she feels as I do, she murmured to herself, *she'll need company for a bit.*

But Mrs. Stafford-Smyth was not feeling at all let down. She was still excited about the party as she welcomed Belinda into her room. "Didn't everything go just fine?" she enthused, and Belinda nodded in response. Aunt Virgie had slipped from her violet gown and into a soft pink robe. Sitting at the vanity, with her gray hair loosened from its pins, she was gently brushing the wispy tresses as she talked to Belinda's reflection in the mirror. Her cheeks were flushed and her voice filled with excitement.

"Celia had a wonderful idea," she began at once. "Just as she was leaving she drew me aside and suggested that I spend some time with her and her sister in New Yawk."

Belinda's eyes widened.

"What do you think of that?" asked the older woman, turning to face Belinda, who could already see what Mrs. Stafford-Smyth thought of it.

"Why, it—it sounds wonderful," Belinda answered, surprised at the sudden turn of events.

"Yes," mused the older woman. "Yes, I think I'd like that. I haven't been to New Yawk for yeahs. Haven't been anywheah for such a long time. I think I'd like that just fine."

"It would be good for you," responded Belinda, feeling a strange turning in the pit of her stomach. *What am I to do in the meantime?* she wondered silently. *Stay in this big house all by myself?*

"I could do some shopping, take in a few plays, heah the orchestra again. Yes, I think I'll accept the invitation."

"And when will you go?" Belinda inquired.

"Next week. There isn't much time, but any shopping that needs doing can be done in New Yawk. It would be exciting to look for a new gown someplace besides LeSouds."

"How long will—?"

"Six weeks," Mrs. Stafford-Smyth cut in. "Six weeks. That should be just right. Long enough that one won't need to rush to get everything done, but not so long as to weah out one's welcome."

Belinda nodded. "You know Aunt Celia's sister well?" asked Belinda.

"Oh my, yes. We were deah, deah friends until she moved to New Yawk. The three of us were always togethah. She's different than Celia—more subdued, more dignified. A real lady in every sense of the word. Lost her husband five yeahs ago. Nevah has recovahed, Celia says. She loves to have company. Celia goes at least once a yeah, but this yeah she has asked for me, too."

"That's nice," smiled Belinda. "The trip will be good for you." She kissed the older woman on the cheek and went to her own room.

But Belinda did not fall asleep very quickly. Her thoughts kept going round and round. What would she *do* all day while her employer was in New York? At times she had felt lonely enough even with Aunt Virgie at home. She wasn't worried now about the older woman's health. Mrs. Stafford-Smyth seemed to be perfectly well again. But Belinda did feel a sense of panic and loss at the thought of being on her own.

Suddenly Belinda sat straight up in bed, a smile spreading over her face in the darkness. *Of course,* she said to herself. *Of course. Why didn't I think of it immediately? I've been aching to go home. This is the perfect opportunity! I won't need to worry about Aunt Virgie while I'm gone.*

Belinda should have lain down and gone directly to sleep then, but she didn't. On and on raced her mind, thinking of home, trying to envision how each person might have changed, thinking of the fun of surprising her friends, cherishing the thought of spending time with her beloved family. It was almost morning before her mind would let her slip off into much-needed sleep.

I'm going home. Home. It's been such a long, long time.

During the next few days the whole house was in an uproar. Mrs. Stafford-Smyth had announced her intentions to her household staff, and everyone was busy with preparations for her departure.

Belinda was perhaps the busiest of all. There was the choosing of Mrs. Stafford-Smyth's wardrobe and the packing, the last-minute shopping for small items, the dusting of hat feathers, and the changing of ribbons. Through it all Belinda flitted back and forth with a smile on her face. Soon she too would be off on her own journey. "Oh, Ma, I can hardly wait!" she whispered joyfully to herself.

One afternoon Windsor entered the sitting room with some garments over his arm. "Madam's cleaning," he informed Belinda in answer to her unasked question. "I shall take it to her at once."

"I'm going up. I'll take it if you wish," Belinda offered.

Windsor had become accustomed to Belinda lending a hand now and then. Still, he had rigid ideas of proper positions and activities for the staff. Belinda was the nurse-companion of his lady. She should not be running errands with the laundry. But after giving the matter some quick thought, he passed the garments to Belinda without argument. Trying to explain would be more difficult than it was worth, he decided.

"Thank you, miss," he said stiffly, and Belinda started off with the clothing, a bit of a smile on her lips.

"Your garments from the cleaners have been returned," she said as she entered the room.

"Oh, good!" exclaimed the woman. "I was beginning to feah that they wouldn't come in time since the owner had said they would be here yesterday."

"Well, they're here now. Should I hang them in the closet or pack them?" Belinda asked.

"I've left room in that trunk for them," responded Mrs. Stafford-Smyth, pointing, and Belinda smiled to herself as she moved toward the chest.

My, she thought to herself, *whatever will she do with all these clothes? And her planning to do more shopping as well! And here I expect to be gone the same length of time and I'm using one suitcase and a hatbox.* Belinda smiled again.

"Do you have youh packing done?" Mrs. Stafford-Smyth asked.

Belinda was surprised at the question but shook her head. "It won't take me long," she assured her.

Mrs. Stafford-Smyth looked a bit alarmed. "Don't short youhself on time," she said anxiously. "The train leaves at ten."

"My train doesn't leave until four," Belinda responded. She had already made the arrangements and purchased her ticket, but at her answer Mrs. Stafford-Smyth stopped mid-stride, her head quickly coming up.

"Whatevah do you mean?" she asked sharply.

Belinda began to flush. It was true that she hadn't asked her employer's permission. She had meant to talk to her about it, but they had just been so busy there had never seemed to be time. Surely the woman hadn't expected her to stay and care for the house. There was Windsor and Potter and the maids. Mrs. Stafford-Smyth had never before left anyone else to oversee the staff when she had traveled. Belinda had just assumed that she would not be needed. But she had been wrong to assume. She should have asked permission before getting her ticket. After all, she was in the employ—

"What do you mean?" Mrs. Stafford-Smyth asked again.

"Oh, Aunt Virgie," began Belinda apologetically. "I'm sorry. I just wasn't thinking. I guess I've been in such a dither. I should have asked you. I didn't realize you expected me to stay on here and—"

"Stay on *heah*? Well, of course not. I expect you to accompany me—to New Yawk."

"Accompany you?" echoed Belinda dumbly.

Mrs. Stafford-Smyth looked shaken. "Of course."

"But—but you didn't say—say anything about me going with you," Belinda reminded the older woman.

"I didn't?" Mrs. Stafford-Smyth looked bewildered. "Maybe I didn't. I guess—I guess I didn't think that it—that anything else would be considered. I just expected you to know. Careless of me. Dreadfully careless."

Belinda's face was white.

"Well, no mattah," went on the woman. "There is still time for you to get ready. I'll call Ella to help you pack," and Mrs. Stafford-Smyth moved toward the bell.

"But—" stammered Belinda. "But I've—I've made other plans."

Mrs. Stafford-Smyth stopped with her hand on the buzzer. "You—you— What plans?" she asked simply.

"I've—I've purchased a ticket—a train ticket for home," Belinda managed.

Mrs. Stafford-Smyth lowered herself into a nearby chair. "I see," she said slowly.

Belinda rushed to her and knelt beside her. "I really didn't know that you expected me to go with you. I thought it was just you and Aunt Celia. I didn't know there was room for more guests than that. So, I decided that it was a good time for me to—to go home for a visit. I'm sorry. I didn't think you'd mind."

Mrs. Stafford-Smyth was pale too. Her hand trembled as she reached out to smooth back Belinda's wayward curls.

"You'll—you won't *stay* home, will you?" she asked shakily.

"Oh, no," promised Belinda quickly. "I just plan to be gone for as long as you'll be away."

Mrs. Stafford-Smyth took a deep breath. "My goodness, child," she said with a nervous laugh. "You nigh scared the breath out of me."

"You didn't think—?" began Belinda, but she realized that it was exactly what Mrs. Stafford-Smyth had thought. Seeing the color gradually return to the older woman's face, Belinda realized just how much it meant to her to have Belinda's company in the big, lonely house.

And with that realization Belinda knew that she could never, never just walk out and leave the woman all alone. The thought sent a sick chill through her body. She loved Mrs. Stafford-Smyth dearly. The older woman was like the grandmother she had never had the chance to know, but to stay with her indefinitely at the expense of never being with the family she loved was a terrible commitment. Belinda didn't know if she could bear it, if she could really be that unselfish.

"You poor child," Mrs. Stafford-Smyth was crooning softly, her hands again smoothing back Belinda's hair. "How thoughtless I've been. Heah I've sat day after day, not even realizing how lonesome you must be foah those you love. And how lonesome they must be for you! Of course you should go home. I should have thought of it myself. It's a perfect opportunity for you. I'm glad you had sense enough to think of it, even if I didn't."

Her hand stopped, resting on Belinda's head. A shadow passed over her face as she looked into Belinda's blue eyes. "And I will not hold you to that promise," she said gently, though her eyes begged Belinda to return. "You know I love you. You know I want you heah, but I will not ask you for such a promise."

"I'll be back, Aunt Virgie," Belinda said in a whisper, and she leaned forward to kiss the older woman on the cheek.

Chapter 4

Home

The whole house was in a turmoil of activity the next morning. Breakfast in the north parlor was a hurried affair, nervous maids fluttering nearby while Mrs. Stafford-Smyth went down a long, long list of last-minute instructions with Potter and Windsor. Windsor nodded glumly from time to time. It was clear he thought that Madam again was showing her streak for foolish gadding about. He did not sanction such travel.

Belinda must have been up and down the stairs a dozen times, running for this, tucking in that, securing this, dusting off that. At long last the carriage with Mrs. Celia Prescott pulled up at the front of the house and Mrs. Stafford-Smyth, bag and baggage, was loaded in for the station.

"My land, girl," exclaimed Mrs. Prescott to Belinda, "where are your hat and gloves?"

"Belinda is not accompanying us," replied Mrs. Stafford-Smyth.

"She's not? Well, whatever will you do—?"

"I will manage just fine," Mrs. Stafford-Smyth put in archly. "I haven't quite forgotten how to cayah for myself."

"But I thought—I just assumed that—"

"Belinda is going to take a trip home to see her family while I am gone," continued Mrs. Stafford-Smyth.

"You'd—you'd let her? She might not be back," argued Mrs. Prescott, and Belinda couldn't help but smile at the genuine

37

warning in the woman's voice. There had been a time when Mrs. Prescott had figured Belinda to be unnecessary and ill-equipped to care for the well-being of her friend, Virginia Stafford-Smyth.

Mrs. Stafford-Smyth drew Belinda to her and kissed her on the forehead. "That is her decision," she said softly. "She knows how much I would miss her."

Unable to say anything, Belinda felt the tears forming in her eyes.

"Goodbye, my deah," said the older woman. "I shall miss you. Tell your mama for me what a blessed woman she is to have such a daughtah."

Belinda swallowed.

"Now you have a good time, you heah. Do all those things you have been missing." She kissed Belinda again. "Bye now."

Belinda managed a goodbye and waved as the carriage pulled out into the street and passed out of sight.

She turned and slowly made her way into the big house. She hadn't even started her own packing yet. Still, she would not need to take much with her. There were many things hanging in her closet at the farm. She would make-do with them.

She was met at the door by Windsor. "Would you like me to summon Ella for you, miss?" he asked Belinda.

Belinda was a bit surprised at his concern.

"I think I can manage fine, thank you," she responded.

"But I know you've been much to busy to care for your own packing," he continued. "Madam always needs so much done before one of her trips—"

"I don't intend to pack much," Belinda assured him. She couldn't help but smile at his carefully worded reference to Madam's choice of travel "necessities." "I left some clothing at home in my closet," she explained. "I can use it while I'm there."

Windsor looked surprised, and then Belinda remembered that it had been almost three years since she had been home. A respectable young lady would certainly not return to fashions of three years past. Belinda smiled again.

"Fashions do not change that much, or that quickly, in my hometown," she assured the butler. "I think that along with the few things I take, I'll manage just fine."

"As you wish, miss," he replied courteously, but she could see he was not really convinced.

To Belinda's surprise it did take her nearly till departure time to complete her preparations. *Wouldn't Ma love to see this pink dress? But then I won't have room for the blue one that matches my eyes,* she debated. Eventually she made all the necessary decisions. The stylish blue hat was carefully tucked in the hatbox along with some extra pairs of white gloves. She took one last look around her room, tidied her dresser and her bathroom and rang for Windsor.

As the butler left her room with her bag and hatbox, Belinda pinned her traveling hat in place and picked up a light wrap. The day was still pleasantly warm, so she would not put it on just yet. She followed Windsor down the steps, smiled a goodbye to the staff who had gathered to see her off and climbed aboard the carriage.

As the team moved down the long, circular lane, Belinda turned for one more look at the big house. *Marshall Manor.* It seemed impossible that she had learned to think of the beautiful place as home.

Then Belinda eagerly turned forward. *No, not home,* she corrected herself. Home was where she was going now. Home was Pa and Ma and Clare and Kate. Home was Arnie and Anne. Home was Luke and Abbie. Home was nieces and nephews who had most likely forgotten who she was and what she had once meant to them. That was home. Belinda held her breath in excitement and anticipation. She could hardly wait to get home—but at the same time she felt a nagging fear.

Will it be the same? Can it possibly be the same? How much has changed? What if—what if—? But Belinda finally made herself stop. She would take things one day at a time. For now she would concentrate on seeing again the faces of those she loved.

Belinda was sure the train trip west to her home was taking many times longer than it had taken to travel east to Boston. *At least it sure seems longer,* she told herself. Each stop, each large city and small town left behind meant that much greater excitement and impatience in Belinda. Sitting on the edge of her seat, she strained to see ahead as far as possible and willed the train to move faster.

She was too agitated to pay much attention to her fellow passengers. Usually she liked to watch people around her. She twisted her hands nervously until her gloves were soiled and wrinkled. *I'm glad I brought extra pairs,* she thought distractedly.

Meals were provided with the ticket, but she had a difficult time eating. But to help pass some time, she did go to the dining car for each mealtime. She even managed a nod and smile when she met an elderly person or a young mother with her children, but certainly not with her usual interest and enthusiasm. Back in her seat, Belinda concentrated on the distant horizon, aching, longing for the train to roll into the familiar station and announce her arrival with a hiss of steam.

The closer she got to home, the more agitated she became. She fidgeted, fretted and fumbled with her purse straps. Only her good manners kept her from pacing the aisle. *Will this trip ever end?* she asked through clenched teeth.

She had notified only Luke. She would have been happy to surprise him also, but it seemed right that someone know of her plans.

"Don't tell the others," she had warned. "I want it to be a secret." Belinda had no reason to think he would give it away. But as she sat twisting and turning on the velvet-covered seat of the passenger car, she wondered if she had done the right thing. *Will the shock be too much for Mama?* she wondered. *How will I get out to the farm? Maybe Luke will be busy with a house call or surgery and not be able to meet the train.*

Belinda's thoughts whirled, fretful with imaginary worries. Had she been childish and silly in her desire for surprise? *Well, it's too late now,* she finally concluded. She could only wait to see how it would all turn out.

And then they passed a familiar farm—they were only a few miles out of town. Belinda's throat was dry and her hands moist. *I'll soon be there. I'll soon be home,* she exulted. She tried to calm her racing heart with deep breaths but it wouldn't be stilled. She leaned back against the seat and closed her eyes, trying to pray. Even her prayer was jumbled.

"Oh, God," she managed, "I'm so excited. So—so dizzy with the thought of being home. I've been *so* lonesome. More lonesome than I even knew. Help me. Help Mama. And Pa. Help me not to shock them too much. And please may they be well. All those I love. I'll—I'll just about die if they've noticeably failed in health since I've been gone. I don't think I could stand it, Lord. Just—just be with us—all of us—and help us to have good days together. And—be with me—and with Mama when the time comes for me to go back to Boston. It'll be hard, Lord. Really hard."

The train blew the whistle—long and loud—and Belinda finished in a rush, "And thanks so much, Lord, for allowing me to come home." Back where her heart had always been. As the wheels churned to a stop, she took a deep breath, gathered her suitcase and hatbox and moved down the aisle toward the exit. Only one other passenger was walking toward the door. *Not many folks get off at this small whistle-stop,* Belinda reminded herself.

And then she was in the open air and down the steps. A kindly porter offered assistance. Stepping onto the wooden platform, she paused to look around and heard her name spoken. There he was—her doctor brother Luke, his arms outstretched toward her as the wind whipped the tails of his coat.

With a glad little cry Belinda ran toward the open arms. "Oh, Luke, Luke" was all she could manage.

They walked from the station together, Luke carrying Belinda's heavy suitcase and she the hatbox. "I didn't dare bring the team," Luke was telling her. "I knew Abbie would ask questions if I harnessed the team to go to the office."

"Oh, the office!" cried Belinda. "I can hardly wait to see your new office."

"But not today," Luke pointed out firmly. "I don't plan to do one thing today except escort you to the family. I could hardly *stand* not telling them, Belinda! Abbie and the kids will be so excited. And then we'll need to get you on home to Ma and Pa. They won't believe their eyes. Just to sorta prepare the way, I told Ma that Abbie and I would be coming out to the farm for supper tonight."

Belinda laughed, thinking how smart Luke had been and how much fun it was going to be.

"I told Jackson that I was taking the rest of the day off. Thankfully he didn't ask why," Luke explained.

At the mention of Jackson, Belinda felt a strange sensation in the pit of her stomach. *Does Jackson still think that I should— that I might care for him?* she wondered. She hoped not.

But Luke was talking.

"By the way, you wouldn't want your old job back, would you?"

At Belinda's questioning look, he hurried on. "No one has said anything yet, but I've the feeling that I might not have my nurse for long."

"Is anything wrong with Flo?" Belinda questioned.

"Oh my, no," laughed Luke. "Unless you consider being in love as something wrong."

"She's in love? That's nice," Belinda smiled, relieved. "So who's the lucky guy? Anyone I know?"

"Quite well, in fact," responded Luke, watching Belinda's face. "Jackson."

"Jackson?" Belinda stopped. The news was quite a shock. And then to Belinda's surprise she realized that it was not only a shock—but a relief. She no longer needed to worry about Jackson. He had found happiness with someone else. She fell in step again with her big brother. "That's nice," she smiled. "Jackson and Flo. I think they'll make a very nice couple."

If Luke had worried how Belinda might take the news, he worried no more. It was clear that Belinda had never considered Jackson as any more than a friend.

"Yes," he grinned at her, "they do make a great couple. We're all happy for them."

Chapter 5

Family

"I don't believe it. I *can't* believe it!" cried Abbie over and over as she held Belinda, laughing and crying at the same time. "You're here. Really here! We had started to think you'd never come back."

Belinda understood immediately that Abbie assumed she was home to stay. She decided there would be plenty of time for explanations about that later. Instead, she returned the warm hug, the tears brimming in her own eyes.

"The youngsters!" cried Abbie. "They'll be so excited to see you. They're in the backyard. Luke, will you—?"

But Luke had already thought of the children and gone to fetch them. In they rushed to see the surprise "visitor" their father had summoned them to see.

Nine-year-old Thomas was still running when he burst through the kitchen door, but he slid to a stop, looking at Belinda in unbelief, and then let out a shriek. "Aunt Belinda!" he cried, but his feet did not leave the spot.

Aaron, seven, pushed forward next to see for himself. He took one look at Belinda, then without missing a step he threw himself headlong at her, his small arms wrapping around her legs, his face buried in her skirts. To everyone's amazement he began to sob.

Belinda, perplexed, reached down to hug the boy. "Aaron, Aaron," she whispered. "Aaron, whatever is wrong?" She pushed him back gently, then lifted him into her arms.

He buried his face against her shoulder. "I—I thought you were never coming back," he cried. "I—I—every day we prayed for you—but you never came home." Belinda just held him and rocked him back and forth. The tears coursed down her own cheeks.

"Shhh. Shhh," she comforted the child. "I'm back. See, I'm back."

Thomas pushed forward and came to wrap his arms around Belinda's waist. She couldn't believe how tall he had grown.

"Thomas," she said, a hand on his mop of brown hair, "look at you. Just look at you. You've grown two feet."

Thomas grinned, a twinkle in his eyes. "I've always had two feet," he countered and the kitchen filled with laughter at his little pun.

Belinda sat down on a kitchen chair, Aaron still on her lap. The emotional storm had passed and he was busily mopping up his face with a checkered handkerchief supplied by his mother. Thomas stood close beside Belinda, carefully studying her face.

"Where's Ruthie?" Belinda asked.

"Pa had to go get her. She went to Muffie's house," Thomas explained.

"Who's Muffie?" asked Belinda innocently. Abbie was clucking her tongue impatiently.

"She's not to go there without permission," she said, irritation in her tone. "She knows that."

"Muffie is a dog," supplied Aaron. "He lives down the street."

Belinda looked at Abbie. *Has Ruthie really gone to visit a dog?* her eyes asked.

"The Larsons—two houses down. They are an older couple—who love children. I think Ruthie would live there if she could. They spoil her something awful." Abbie shook her head. "They have a little dog. Ruthie uses that as her excuse to—"

Just then the back door opened and Luke entered, the errant Ruthie by the hand. Her parents exchanged glances. Discipline would need to be meted out—but not at the moment, they seemed to agree. They would deal with the infraction later.

Ruthie, suddenly shy, was too young to remember her Aunt Belinda, though Thomas and Aaron had certainly kept her posted about the fact that she had such an aunt. She clasped her father's hand more tightly and twisted herself behind him.

Thomas urged her to come over. "This is Aunt Belinda," he prompted, tapping Belinda on the shoulder. Aaron's arm tightened possessively around Belinda's neck.

Ruthie finally was coaxed to release her hold on her father and took hesitant steps toward Belinda. Her head was slightly down, her tongue tucked into a corner of her mouth. Shyly she moved forward, and Belinda wondered how she would manage to hold another child. She reached a hand toward Ruthie. The child took it and lowered her eyes, twisting her little shoulders back and forth in embarrassment as she stood before them. Aaron pulled her in close.

"It's our Aunt Belinda," he explained. " 'Member? We told you 'bout her. She's nice. She's home now."

Ruthie managed a shy smile. She even allowed a small hug.

"Ruthie doesn't remember me like you do," Belinda informed Aaron. "She was still so tiny when I left. Just a baby really."

Thomas cut in excitedly, "Does Grandma know you're here?" Belinda shook her head.

Thomas swung back to his father. "Can we take her out, Pa? Can we? Just think how s'prised Grandma's gonna be."

Aaron scrambled off Belinda's lap so quickly she feared he was falling and grabbed for the boy. But he landed on his feet— *like a cat,* Belinda thought—and joined with Thomas in pleading for a trip to the farm. Even young Ruthie began to clap her hands and to beg.

"Hush. Hush, all of you," Luke laughed, holding up his hands. "Of course we'll take Aunt Belinda to the farm. But first she needs to catch her breath. Now I suggest we let her freshen up a bit while your mama puts on the tea. We'll have tea together, and then we'll all go to the farm. I told Grandma we'd be out to join her for supper."

Three children cheered loudly, and Belinda was tempted to place her hands over her ears. Instead, she chuckled to herself,

It certainly was never this noisy at Marshall Manor!

"Thomas, could you hand me that hatbox, please?" Belinda asked.

"You already have a hat on," Aaron reminded her, looking at her curiously.

Belinda laughed. "Yes, I know," she admitted.

"You're going to put it in the box?" asked Thomas.

"Well, that would be a good idea too, but right now I'm looking for something. . . ." Belinda searched the interior for a moment and came up with a bag of peppermints. "These are for all of you to share," she said, passing the bag of candy to Abbie. "Your mama will pass them out as she wishes."

Three sets of eyes brightened and three pairs of hands reached toward Abbie. She allowed one candy per child and tucked the rest safely away in the cupboard. As Belinda left the room to go wash, she heard Luke begin his discussion with Ruthie.

"Now, young lady, what has your mama told you about running off to see Muffie without asking her for permission?" he began.

Belinda heard a little sob from the girl.

Oh, dear, she thought as she went into the bathroom and removed her hat to tidy her hair and wash her hands and face. *I'm glad it's not me who has to discipline. It must be so much easier to just blink at some things.*

But Luke would not do that, easy as it would have been. "Discipline needs to be consistent," she had often heard Luke say, "or it is not discipline—only punishment." And she knew her brother Luke did not believe in punishment for its own sake.

Belinda's excitement matched the children's during the ride to the farm. Thomas, Aaron and Ruthie all talked constantly, vying for her attention and pointing out every farm and landmark along the way. Belinda could have named them all herself, but she allowed them the fun of being her "tour guides."

The nearer they came to the farm, the harder Belinda's heart pounded. *Have I done the right thing? Should I have warned the folks of my coming?* she debated within herself again. *What if the shock—?* She took a deep breath and tried to concentrate on the children's chatter, grasping the buggy seat until her knuckles turned white. Luke was already pressing the team as fast as safety would allow.

And then they were turning down the long lane. Belinda had always thought of the white farmhouse as large. She was surprised at how small it looked to her now—small compared to Marshall Manor. Small and quite simple.

But it is home, she exulted—familiar and loved. Belinda edged forward on the seat and could scarcely wait for the buggy to stop.

"Now don't you holler out anything to Grandma," Luke warned the children. "Aunt Belinda wants to surprise her." They nodded in wide-eyed understanding, and Ruthie clapped a hand over her own mouth "just in case."

The farm dog welcomed them, even seeming to remember Belinda. He stopped at her side long enough to lick her hand and wag his tail, and she patted his head fondly. "You remember me, don't you?" she murmured with satisfaction. Then the dog scampered away, far more interested in the children who ran on ahead to the house.

Marty appeared at the door, drying her hands on her apron. "You're earlier than I expected," she called. "How did you get away from the office so soon?" She leaned down to hug Aaron and Ruthie. "How's school, Thomas?" she inquired.

Belinda, screened behind Luke and Abbie, could hardly contain herself. She wished to rush headlong into her mother's arms. She suppressed the urge and swallowed away a sob from her throat.

"Ready," whispered Luke, and Belinda nodded, tears in her eyes and a smile on her lips. The three adults moved toward the farmhouse. Marty was still busy chatting with the three youngsters. Belinda could hardly believe they hadn't even suggested they had a surprise for Grandma, though they were casting furtive glances toward the approaching adults.

Belinda had almost reached her mother when wee Ruthie could keep quiet no longer. "Look!" she exclaimed, pointing a pudgy finger at Belinda.

Marty looked up. Luke, quick to react, stepped aside at just that minute.

Belinda heard Marty's gasp. With a cry of "My baby" she threw herself toward her youngest. Belinda met her halfway and, weeping, they wrapped their arms around each other. Marty was whispering words of love and endearment over and over, but she was saying "Belinda" now, not "baby." Belinda did not remember her mother calling her that before. *Is that really how she thinks of me?* she wondered for a moment.

"Oh, Mama," Belinda finally managed, "I'm so glad to see you!"

Marty pulled a handkerchief from her apron pocket and wiped her eyes and nose. She held Belinda at arms' length and studied her face carefully. "You've changed," she said at last. "But I see nothing but maturity in your face. You've grown up, Belinda," and she hugged her close again.

For Belinda's part, her mother looked very much the same as she remembered her. *Thank you, Lord,* she whispered. *Thank you for taking good care of Mama.*

The rest of the family demanded equal time, and the two women were forced to draw apart while all the children tried to talk at once.

"Were you surprised, Grandma? Were you surprised?"

"Well—my lands! I guess I was."

"It was a good trick, wasn't it, Grandma? We really fooled you, didn't we?"

"You certainly did. You certainly did. My, my," and Marty cast a loving glance toward Belinda, "it was a good surprise." And she led the way into the big farm kitchen.

"Grandpa will be surprised, too, won't he? Won't he?"

"He will. He sure will."

And so the talk went on, bubbling and humming around her until Belinda felt her head was fairly spinning.

"I'm gonna run and tell Uncle Clare and Aunt Kate," shouted Thomas and headed for the door, then slid to a stop and looked toward Belinda. "Can I?"

"Go ahead," laughed Belinda. "They might as well hear it from you, and I am anxious to see them all."

The house was in even more confusion when Kate and the boys arrived. Only two of the nephews were home. Dan was off with his father on a farm errand. Belinda was startled to note that David was taller than she was and Dack was very quickly catching up. They gave her boyish hugs and Kate held her fiercely. Belinda wondered if Kate was really thinking of her own Amy Jo as she hugged so tightly.

"What do you hear from Amy Jo?" Belinda asked when she could draw a breath.

"She's fine, she says. Expectin' her second child any day now." Kate wiped her eyes, drew a deep breath and managed a smile. "Her first little one will soon be three. Hard to believe, isn't it?"

Belinda nodded, imagining lively Amy Jo as a mother.

"Well, that's the way life is," shrugged Kate. "Ya raise 'em to leave. That's what life is about. Dan now, he's got a girl. A nice girl, too, so I s'pect it won't be long till he'll be off on his own as well."

"Is Dan—is Dan still working with—with Rand?" Belinda couldn't believe the difficulty she was having with the simple question.

"Oh, no," explained Kate quickly. "Rand left. He went back to the town—wherever it was—where he lived before. Dan does odd little building jobs for the neighbors, but mostly he farms with his pa."

Belinda was relieved. Her trip home would not be marred by another confrontation with Rand, though she could have enjoyed a visit with him.

"Rand married a girl from down there," Kate went on. "She didn't want to leave her family, so they settled in the area."

Jackson—and now Rand, Belinda mused, her eyes reflecting her surprise.

But no one noticed, and Dack cut into the conversation. "Are you going to be a nurse again?" he asked Belinda.

"I'm a nurse now," Belinda answered. All eyes turned to Belinda as she spoke. "In fact, I did a good deal of nursing the early part of the summer. I wrote Mama—Grandma—about it. Aunt Virgie—Mrs. Stafford-Smyth—was very sick. I was afraid we might even lose her."

"You call her Aunt Virgie?" asked Marty.

"Yes, she asked me to," Belinda stated simply, and Marty nodded.

"Is she better now?" asked Marty.

"Much better, though it took her quite a while to get over it. But she's fine now. Just fine. In fact, she's feeling so well that she's off to New York for six weeks."

Marty looked at Belinda, her eyes shadowed. She did not speak out loud, but Belinda could feel the words pass between them. *And while she's in New York, you have come home?* Marty's eyes asked. The question was so real Belinda almost nodded solemnly in answer.

And you will go back to Boston? Marty's questioning eyes probed, and Belinda answered that within herself too.

Marty turned her head then, and Belinda expected it was to hide her tears of disappointment.

Thomas drew their attention. "When's Grandpa coming home, Grandma?"

Marty's eyes traveled to the clock on the kitchen shelf. "Soon," she replied evenly. "He should be here soon."

And then the farm dog barked an excited welcome, and they all knew that Clark was on his way.

Chapter 6

Seeing Pa

Belinda was so emotionally drained that she knew she could not bear another "game." Before anyone could urge her to duck in the pantry or slip into the living room, she rose from her chair and rushed out the door.

The big team hadn't even pulled to a stop in front of the barn before Clark's attention fastened on someone flying toward him, arms outstretched.

"Pa," she called in a half sob. "Pa."

Clark looked in wonder, unable to comprehend what his eyes—and ears—were telling him. And then he flung the reins from his hands, flipped himself over the wheel and met his girl—his Belinda—with open arms.

"It's you. It's really you," he murmured huskily into her hair as he lifted her from the ground and gently swung her back and forth. Belinda wondered if her ribs might be crushed in the bear hug.

"Oh, Pa," she laughed as she kissed his cheek. "Pa—it's so good to see you."

He set her back on her feet and looked deeply into her eyes. "How ya be?" he asked sincerely.

"Fine—just fine," Belinda assured him.

He hugged her to himself again, tears unheeded on his cheeks.

Belinda reached out to set his hat, dislodged in his quick

descent from the wagon, back on straight. "Oh, Pa" was all she could say.

"Ya look great. Jest great," he told her.

Belinda laughed. "Not really," she said ruefully. "I can feel my hair slipping over my ears, my dress is wrinkled, my face feels flushed. Why, I must look a sight."

Clark laughed heartily. "Ya look good to me," he insisted. "When did ya git here?"

"I came in on the train. Luke brought me out."

"Luke knew?" asked Clark, and Belinda nodded.

"The rascal! Never said a word—unless he told yer ma."

"No—he didn't tell anyone. I asked him not to. But—but I later wished that—that I hadn't been so secretive. It wasn't fair—not really."

"Well, yer here now—thet's what matters," Clark responded and gave her another hug and a kiss on the forehead.

David arrived then. "I'll take care of the team, Grandpa," he offered.

"Thanks, boy," Clark responded, and he motioned toward the house. Belinda allowed herself to be led, her pa's arm still around her waist.

He wanted to ask her about her plans, but he checked himself. There was plenty of time for that. No use spoiling the moment. He feared she might not be home to stay. But surely Marty had already asked her. He'd get his news from Marty. Later.

"How's your patient? Mrs.—let's see—Mrs. Stafford-Smyth. She doin' okay?"

"She's fine—now," responded Belinda. "She got over her flu just fine. She's off to New York for six weeks. Staying with a friend."

And then Clark knew. *Six weeks—not long. Not long at all,* he thought. But perhaps they shouldn't take lightly even small blessings. She was home now. They would enjoy every minute. His arm tightened about his youngest.

"How have you been keeping?" Belinda asked solicitously.

"Fine," responded Clark. "Don't I look fine?"

"You look just great," laughed Belinda. "I don't think you've aged a bit. Oh, a few more gray hairs," she teased, "but other than that—"

"Thet gray hair," said Clark, removing his hat and running fingers through his still-heavy head of hair, "thet comes from havin' young'uns scattered all over the country from east to west."

Belinda laughed.

"What'd yer ma say when she seen ya?" Clark asked next. "Bet she was fit to be tied."

Belinda grinned, then sobered. "I sure hope it wasn't too foolish of me to come sneaking in," she replied. "But she seems to have handled it very well."

"Good," said Clark as he held the door for her.

They were met by a barrage of shouts, all the children talking at once. Luke had held them in check so Belinda could have a few moments alone with her father, but now they all wanted to get in on the excitement.

"Surprise, Grandpa! Surprise! Weren't you surprised? Wasn't it a good trick? We already knew. We already knew! Weren't you surprised?"

Clark tried to answer but was drowned out. He held up his hand—his family signal for some order. When the clamoring had turned to a soft hum, he answered their eager questions.

"It was a grand surprise," he informed them. "I never had me the faintest idea thet Belinda was comin' home. It sure was a great surprise. Why, ya couldn't have brought me a better one—an' thet's a fact."

They were about to return to their excited babbling, but Clark again held up a hand. "Now, I need me a cup o' coffee— to sorta get over my shock—like, iffen Grandma has one handy."

Marty smiled, nodded, and moved to the stove.

"She might even have some cookies and milk fer hungry little people," Clark went on, "seein' as how it's too early fer supper yet. I s'pose she'd let ya have 'em on the back veranda."

Kate went to help get the cookies and milk ready for the children, and Marty hurried to cut some date loaf. She wished she had some of Belinda's favorite lemon cake on hand. *Iffen*

54

I'd only knowed . . . she found herself thinking, and then dismissed the idea. *If I'd knowed ahead, I'd likely made myself a'most sick with the excitement of it all.*

Belinda moved to the cupboard. The cups were still in the same place. It was nice to come home and find so many things—and people—unchanged. Belinda poured the steaming coffee into the cups and then went to the pantry for the cream and sugar. They, too, were in their usual spot. Belinda smiled. She could just slip right in at home again and carry on as though she'd never been away. A nice thought.

The commotion subsided considerably with the children out of the kitchen. It seemed like such a long, long time since Belinda had sat at the familiar table, with familiar folks, talking over simple and familiar topics.

She was brought up-to-date on each family member, told news of neighbors, updated on the affairs of the church and reminded of things from the past. Belinda wished they could just chatter on and on, but Marty broke the spell.

"My lands!" she gasped, staring at the clock. "Look at the time. Why, we'll never be havin' our supper iffen I don't get me busy."

Kate jumped up and moved toward the kitchen door. "Clare'll soon be home," she scolded herself.

"Why don't ya jest join us?" Marty invited. "I have a roast in the oven—thet's the one thing I did do on time. We'll make it stretch."

"I've got a couple pies," Kate responded. "I can bring 'em over."

Marty nodded. "I baked jest one today," she answered. "Yer two sure would help."

"I'll fix a salad too," said Kate on her way out.

Marty nodded again, then called to Kate, "Do you s'pose you could send David over to Arnie's? They should be told. Tell Anne to bring what she has an' come to supper iffen she wishes—or else come over as soon as they can after supper."

Belinda smiled, soon to be reunited with her family. At least all who lived nearby. Missy and Willie, Ellie and Lane and all their offspring were still far away in the West. Nandry and Clae and their children weren't close enough to join them either. But the ones Belinda had grown up with, the family near home— she would soon see them all. *It's so good to be home again!* she breathed.

Late that night the last team left for home. Kate reluctantly lifted her light shawl from the coat rack. "I guess we'd better get on home too," she sighed. "The boys still have 'em school in the mornin'."

"Aw. Do we hafta?" protested Dack.

"I'll be here when you come home again tomorrow," Belinda reminded him.

"This is David's last year," Kate informed Belinda. "He's our scholar. Likes school much better'n the others ever have. Never have to coax David to get him up in the mornin's," she finished proudly.

"What's he planning?" asked Belinda.

"Hasn't decided, but he'd like to go on fer further schoolin'."

"Good for him," Belinda nodded, pleased about David and happy for Kate.

The last goodbyes were said, and Belinda settled back at the table with Clark and Marty, still lingering over coffee cups.

"I s'pose yer awful tired?" commented Marty, touching Belinda's cheek softly.

"I am. It's the excitement, I guess. And I couldn't sleep well on the train at all. It rumbles and groans all night long. But, really, it was the thought of coming home that kept me from relaxing."

Marty took Belinda's hand, squeezing it slightly as her eyes filled with tears. "Iffen I had knowed ya were comin'," she admitted, "I wouldn't have been doin' any sleepin' either."

Clark chuckled. "An' thet's the truth," he agreed.

Belinda decided that maybe her plan of coming home unannounced had not been so foolish after all.

"Arnie looks good," Belinda commented. "Looks even better than he did when I left."

Marty nodded. "Finally got his problems worked out an' his

bitterness taken care of," she acknowledged. "Bitterness can age one like nothin' else can."

"It's a fact," nodded Clark. "'Most made an old man of 'im fer a time."

"His Abe's arm looks good," continued Belinda. "Not nearly as twisted as it was. Why, folks wouldn't even notice it much anymore. One can almost forget he ever had that encounter with the bull."

"Three surgeries it took." Marty shook her head, remembering. "Three surgeries to straighten it out agin. But worth it—every one of 'em. Arnie can see thet now—but my—it was a struggle fer 'im to let the boy go under the surgeon's knife."

"I'm so glad he finally consented," Belinda commented.

"Ya wantin' more coffee?" Marty asked suddenly.

"No. No thanks. I've had plenty." Belinda laughed lightly. "I guess Aunt Virgie and I have taken more to drinking tea. I'm not so used to much coffee anymore."

"Well, I sure can fix a pot of tea," Marty replied, jumping up from her chair.

"Mama," Belinda said quickly, reaching out a restraining hand to her mother, "I don't need tea either. Why, I've been eating and drinking ever since I set foot in the door. I won't be able to move in six weeks if—" Belinda stopped.

The shadow darkened Marty's eyes again. "Six weeks, is it?" she asked slowly.

Belinda nodded, toying with her cup.

"I feared as much," said Marty. She pushed her cup back listlessly, no longer interested in coffee.

"It's—it's that I can't—can't feel comfortable just leaving her," Belinda began, sensing that some kind of explanation was needed. "She—she is so alone. She really has no one—no family who cares about her. Her grandsons are in France, and she gets so lonely. I can see it in her face. I . . . I . . ." Belinda faltered to a stop.

" 'Course," said Clark, reaching for Belinda's hand.

"Is there—is there—anyone special in the city?" Marty asked.

Belinda smiled, but shook her head.

"Ya know," Marty remarked slowly, "it really would be easier iffen there was. I mean—fer me. Ya wouldn't seem so—so alone then."

Belinda was surprised at her mother's comment but understood. "I'm not an old maid yet, Mama," she reassured Marty with a smile.

"We-ll," responded Marty, "yer not gittin' any younger either. All the other girls was—" Marty dropped the sentence. Belinda well knew her sisters had married when they were much younger than she was now.

"No one ever said thet everybody has to marry," Marty quickly amended. "Thet's somethin' thet each person has to decide fer herself."

Belinda nodded.

"It's not so much I want ya married. It's jest I don't want ya all alone an' lonely—ya understand?"

Belinda nodded again. Marty reached over and patted the hand Clark was still holding.

"Are ya lonely?"

Marty's question surprised Belinda. For a moment she could not answer. A lump in her throat threatened to choke her. She blinked back tears and nodded slowly.

"Sometimes," she admitted, dropping her head. "Sometimes I get dreadfully lonesome. I'd come home—so fast—if I could see my way clear to do it."

Belinda lifted her face to look from her mother to her father. Their eyes were wet as well.

Marty patted the hand again.

"Well, ya know what ya gotta do—an' ya know thet ya can come home agin—anytime—anytime ya be wantin' to."

Belinda fumbled for her handkerchief. "I know," she nodded. "And that keeps me going during the really lonely times. Thanks. Thanks—both of you."

For a moment their eyes held, and then Marty pushed back from the table. "An' now you'd best be off ta bed afore ya fall off yer chair," she urged. "Yer pa and me have kept ya up long enough. We needn't say everything tonight. We have six weeks to catch us up."

"You have anything thet needs carryin' up?" asked Clark, rising from the table.

"Luke took my suitcase up," answered Belinda.

"Ya go on then," Marty continued. "Yer room should be ready fer ya. I dusted and freshened it up just last week. I'll jest gather these few cups in the dishpan. We'll be right up ourselves—yer pa and me."

Belinda kissed them both and climbed the familiar steps to her room. The door stood ajar, the suitcase at the foot of the bed.

She entered the room and stood looking about her. It was a simple room. The bed was still covered with the same spread Belinda remembered so well. At the window the matching curtains breathed in and out with the slight movement of the night air. Braided rugs scattered here and there brightened the plainness of the wooden floors. Belinda couldn't help but remember that at one time she had considered this bedroom the most beautiful in the world.

It was still very special, in a homey sort of way. She smiled as she crossed to the bed and turned down the blanket, fluffing up the pillow. She would sleep like a baby back in her own bed. Belinda yawned and began unpacking before retiring.

But after three years the bed seemed reluctant to mold to her unfamiliar form, and tired as she was, the clock downstairs had chimed twice before Belinda was finally able to forget the events of the day and settle down to sleep.

Chapter 7

Adjustments

Belinda awakened to the crowing of the farm roosters, the bellowing of the cows, and the clatter from the farmyard. She didn't mind. She didn't want to waste precious time in bed anyway. She threw back the blankets and eased herself up, thinking to hurriedly care for her toilet before choosing what she would wear for the day.

But as she poised, one foot reaching for a slipper, she remembered with a start that there was no bathroom in the farmhouse. She would have to dress first. She would need to wash in the kitchen—to carry and heat water when she wanted a bath.

She hurried to her closet to choose from the dresses that had remained behind when she left for the East. She intended to pick something homey—something simple for her day about the farm. A simple calico or gingham would take the place of her city silks or satins. Belinda immediately spotted a blue print, one of her favorite dresses. Excitedly she pulled it toward her, then stared in bewilderment.

Is it really this—this simple, this childish? Why, it looks like a dress belonging to a little girl, she thought, astonished. *Surely—surely I was more grown-up than that when I left the farm. After all, it's only been three years,* she reasoned. *Was I really wearing such—such tasteless things before going to Boston?*

Soberly Belinda rehung the dress in the closet and pulled out another one. But she was even more shocked as she studied it. One after the other, she assessed each dress left in her closet. *There really isn't a fit one in the lot* was her judgment.

What do Kate and Abbie wear? Belinda found herself asking. *Do they really look as—as old-fashioned as this? Have I just not noticed it before?*

Belinda pictured Kate at their family dinner last night. Yes, Kate did dress very simply, in country frocks much like Marty wore. Belinda had never given it a thought before—but they were dreary, out-of-fashion, though little different from what the other community women wore.

Now Abbie usually wears brighter things—dresses with a bit more taste and style, Belinda thought. But even Abbie, though one of the best-dressed young women in their small town, was not what the ladies of Boston would have considered fashionable.

Belinda had never been conscious of fashion before living in Boston, and even during her time there, she had been totally unaware that she had developed an eye for style.

The thought upset her. *Am I getting proud and—and stuffy?* she asked herself impatiently, and she pulled the blue frock from her closet and tossed it on her bed.

It's a perfectly good dress, she scolded herself. *It's certainly more suitable for farm wear than anything I brought with me.* She slipped her frilly nightdress over her head and put on the simple frock before she could change her mind.

The dress still fit—after a fashion. Belinda noticed with chagrin that it didn't quite fit like it had before. Though she had gained no weight over the past few years, the dress was a bit snug in places. Belinda fretted and pulled, but there was no give. At last she tied up the sash, adjusted the collar and proceeded down the stairs.

Marty was in the kitchen at the big black stove. The room already felt hot to Belinda, and it was just early morning. *Whatever will it be like by nightfall?* she found herself wondering. The early fall weather could still be very warm during the day.

"My, you look nice," Marty beamed at Belinda. She knew

that Marty enjoyed seeing her back in her old flowered blue calico. Belinda didn't trust herself to comment. She feared her voice might give away her true feelings about the wardrobe upstairs.

"I'll be right back," she informed her mother and set out down the path at the back of the house. It had been a long time since she had used an outside facility, and she found it strangely disagreeable.

When she returned, Marty was dishing up a platter of scrambled eggs and farm sausage. "Pa said to call him in as soon as you were up," Marty informed Belinda. "Would you like to call 'im? He's at the spring."

Belinda nodded, looking forward to a quick morning walk to the spring. It had always been one of her favorite spots—just as it had been her mother's. She nodded again and turned to leave.

"Tell 'im everything is ready," Marty called after her, and Belinda took it as a signal that she was to hurry.

It really wasn't far to the spring, but she ran anyway. She would have enjoyed a leisurely walk so she could smell the fall flowers and enjoy the colors of the leaves. She would walk the path again later—many times, perhaps—and enjoy the smells and the colors to her heart's content.

Just as Marty had said, Clark was there, raking fallen leaves from the crystal water.

"Pa," Belinda called, out of breath, "Mama says that breakfast is ready."

Clark looked up from his task.

"My, don't ya look bright and pretty," he responded. Belinda just smiled. Both Clark and Marty seemed to prefer having their little girl back.

"Sleep well?" asked Clark as he set aside the rake.

Belinda wished he hadn't asked. "Well . . ." she hesitated. "It took a long time for me to drop off," she admitted, then quickly added when she saw worry in Clark's eyes, "Guess I was just too excited."

Clark nodded. "A lot happened in one short day," he agreed.

They walked to the house, Belinda almost running to keep

up with the long strides of her pa. "My," she joked, "how fast did you walk when you had two good legs?"

Clark chuckled. "Not much faster, I s'pect. I figured as how I wouldn't let the loss of a limb slow me down any more'n I could help."

"Well, it sure hasn't," panted Belinda.

Clark slowed a bit to accommodate her. "I was jest thinkin' as I was cleanin' the spring," he said slowly, "of thet boy Drew."

Belinda's eyes flickered toward her father. She felt the color strangely rise in her cheeks.

"Ya ever hear from 'im?" asked Clark.

Belinda shook her head.

"He was over a while back," Clark went on. "Called on yer ma an' me."

Belinda looked at her father, her eyes wide with wonder.

"He's home?" she asked softly.

"Was. Ain't no more. He was jest visitin' his ma fer a spell. His pa passed on, ya know."

"No," said Belinda. "No—I didn't know that. What happened?"

"Not sure. Some said heart. It was sudden-like."

"I'm sorry," Belinda responded, her voice not more than a whisper.

"Yeah, it was a shame. A real shame. An' as far as we know, him not ever makin' any move toward the church's teaching either. The missus now, she comes regular-like. Been comin' the last two years. Took a stand about her faith in front of the whole congregation. Really somethin', her bein' sech a quiet, sensitive soul."

"What about the—the younger boy?" asked Belinda. "The one who was going to school?"

"Sidney?"

"Yes—I'd forgotten his name."

"He's still with his ma. Works in town at the feed mill. Rides home every night. Folks say he had his heart set on going fer more education—but he hasn't gone, least not yet."

They were nearing the house. Belinda hadn't asked the questions she really wanted to ask. *What about Drew? Is he still following the Lord? Did he ever become a lawyer as he'd dreamed? Will he ever come back—home? Has he—has he married?* But Belinda asked none of them. Instead she said, "I'll bet Drew's ma was glad to have him home."

There's a nostalgic sound to her voice, Clark thought, but then they were all feeling a bit of nostalgia today. "Yeah," he agreed. "Yeah, she sure was, all right. Sid said thet it was real hard fer her to let 'im go agin."

Clark held the door for Belinda and she passed into the big farm kitchen. On the table a steaming plate of pancakes sent waves of warmth upward. The scrambled eggs and sausage, along with the coffee already poured and waiting beside their plates, added to the delicious breakfast smells.

Hurriedly father and daughter washed for breakfast, using the corner washstand and the big blue basin. Belinda had not shared a towel for ages and it was a rather unfamiliar experience for her now.

Turning again to the heavily laden table, she looked at the syrups, the jams, the jellies. Then her gaze went back to the pancakes and the egg platter. *How in the world will I manage such a breakfast? Does Mama really expect me to eat like a farmhand?* Belinda had become used to scones or tea biscuits or, at the most, a muffin with fruit—and now—She crossed to her plate.

"Ya wantin' some porridge to start with?" asked Marty, adding quickly, "It's yer favorite."

To start with? echoed Belinda silently. *Oh, my!*

Marty didn't hear Belinda's little gasp.

"A—a very small helping, please," smiled Belinda. "I—I haven't done anything to work up an appetite yet."

Clark smiled. "Well, we'll right that quick enough," he teased. "I got some hay thet needs forkin' this mornin'."

Belinda just smiled and bowed her head for the table grace.

After breakfast they had their family devotions together as they'd always done for as long as Belinda could remember. It was wonderful to hear her father read Scripture again. His voice trembled with emotion as he read the stories that to some became commonplace. Belinda loved to hear him read. He had always made the Bible come alive for her.

It was Marty's turn for the morning prayer, and Belinda's thoughts traveled across the country with her as she presented each one of her children and grandchildren to her Lord, asking for His guidance and protection for another day. It was a lengthy prayer. Clark and Marty never hurried their morning devotions.

Afterward Clark pushed back from the table and reached for his hat. Marty waved Belinda aside as she rose to clear the table.

"Now I want you to jest take the day and git reacquainted with yer home," Marty told her.

"But I'm not that rushed for time," Belinda objected. "I'm to be here for six weeks. I can certainly help with the dishes and—"

"No, no," argued Marty. "I've nothin' else to do this mornin'. You jest run along."

Belinda at last agreed. "I guess I'll go back to the spring then and finish the raking," she told Marty. "Pa wasn't quite done when I called him for breakfast."

Marty smiled. "I think thet rakin' the leaves from the spring be one of yer pa's favorite tasks," she said softly. "In the fall he does it every few days. It's a good thing thet the wind always favors 'im by puttin' more leaves back in. I think yer pa enjoys the gurgle an' the talkin' of the stream. But I don't think he'll mind sharin' the pleasure with you."

Belinda smiled in answer.

"'Course, it's my favorite spot, too," Marty admitted. "Always did feel thet I could do my best thinkin' there. An' prayin'," she added without apology.

Belinda understood. The running water had the same effect on her. She had to admit to herself that she was going to the spring now not so much to rake leaves as to think—to recall.

Thoughtfully she walked down the path again, and when she reached the stream she took up the rake leaning against the tree where Clark had left it. She dipped it dreamily into the clear, clean water, wondering as usual how the stream stayed so sparkling, and pulled a few wayward leaves toward the bank.

So Drew has been home, her thoughts began. *It seems such a long, long time since I've seen him—such a long time since I've even heard anything about him. Why, Drew left when I was only seventeen. I'd almost forgotten that Andrew Simpson existed. Almost!* She stopped raking and stared off into the distance.

Yet—yet he kissed me—once—so long ago. We were just children then. I was only sixteen. It was my first kiss. Such a—such a tender, childlike kiss. Like one good friend kissing another. And I thought about it—day and night—for what seemed like forever.

But it's strange—after that kiss, instead of drawing us together, it seemed to drive us apart. Like we both felt embarrassed and didn't know how our feelings should be handled. We only mumbled greetings when we met and avoided looking at each other.

Belinda flushed even now as she thought about it, and then she smiled openly. *We were such—such kids,* she admitted. *Both liking one another, yet afraid to let it show.*

She bent to trail her fingers in the icy water. It helped some to state the truth, even to herself. She had never, ever shared with anyone just how much she had really cared for Drew.

Well, I guess he really didn't feel the same about me was her next thought as she straightened up again, *or he surely would have tried to stay in touch—some way.*

With a sigh Belinda scooped out another batch of leaves and deposited them on the shore.

But what if—what if we had both been visiting home at the same time? What if—what if we had suddenly met on the street in town? Would there have been any kind of feeling for each other after all these years? Belinda couldn't help but wonder.

And then she reminded herself that perhaps Drew was married. She hadn't asked her father. It certainly seemed that Drew was settled—wherever he was now living. He had just come home to visit his ma, her pa had said. That didn't sound like he had plans to ever come back to the area.

Belinda stirred restlessly. *Maybe thinking back isn't such a good idea after all.* She finished and leaned the rake back up against the tree and moved on to explore other favorite places of the farm.

Chapter 8

Memories

It didn't take Belinda long to visit all her old farm haunts. The first place she went was to her pa's barn. She hoisted her skirts and nimbly climbed to the barn loft to check for a new batch of kittens. She would be terribly disappointed if there were none. But after a short search, she discovered their hideaway in a distant corner.

As far as Belinda could tell, there were three in the litter, but they were as wild and unapproachable as young foxes. She never did get anywhere near them, though she tried to coax them to her for a good half hour.

"Now, if I'd been here," she informed the tabby cat, "I'd have had those kittens of yours licking my fingers and playing in my lap long before their eyes were ever open."

Totally unimpressed, the cat said nothing. She also was too wary to let Belinda near her. The mother herself had likely grown up without being handled, Belinda supposed. She finally gave up and climbed down the ladder.

She then spent some time looking for hidden hens' nests. She and Amy Jo had always enjoyed the little game, arguing over which one was the better at out-guessing the farmyard flock.

Belinda found two nests with a total of eleven eggs. She shook them cautiously to test them, concluding that neither hen had been inclined to "set." Belinda bundled the eggs in her

67

skirt and took them to the house to Marty.

Belinda next chose a favorite book and went to the garden
swing. She had intended to read, but with the gentle swaying
of the swing, memories of her childhood companions, Amy Jo
and Melissa, came to her so strongly that she couldn't concentrate.

Why do things have to change? she asked herself unreason-
ably. *Why couldn't we have just stayed in our innocence, our
childish bliss?* But even as she asked, she knew the answer. As
it was, they had felt that they were growing up way too slowly.
Each of them, in her own way, had ached and longed to become
an adult. And now her beloved nieces, Melissa and Amy Jo,
were both hundreds of miles away, with homes of their own.
And she, Belinda, was here only for a short time—as a visitor.
Her duties lay many miles away, too.

The sad, nostalgic thoughts drove Belinda from the swing.
She laid aside the book and wandered to the garden.

Belinda noticed that Marty's apple trees were bearing well.
She could see where Marty had already picked some from this
stem and that. Perhaps the apples had been baked in the pies
Belinda had enjoyed the evening before.

She passed on to the flowers. The goldenrod glowed brightly
in the fall sunshine and the asters lifted proud heads, their
colors varied and vibrant. *"Vibrant,"* thought Belinda. *Vibrant.
Amy Jo used to use that word for just about everything. She'd
found it in one of Melissa's books, and she loved the sound of it.*
Belinda smiled to herself. It seemed like such a long, long time
ago.

That's what I should have done with my six weeks, she suddenly told herself. *I should have gone to see Amy Jo and Melissa.*

But even as she thought of it, she knew better. *Mama and
Pa would've never forgiven me,* she decided, *if I'd gone west
instead of coming here.* Then she admitted, *Really, I wouldn't
have liked it either.*

She moved on, admiring Marty's flowers. *They are pretty,*
she mused, *though nothing like Thomas's tailored flower beds.*

What's the matter with me? Belinda thought crossly. *When
I'm in Boston, I'm longing for the farm; and when I'm on the*

farm, I'm secretly longing for Boston. Don't I fit in anywhere anymore?

The thought was an alarming one—and Belinda had no answer.

She decided to go back to the kitchen. Perhaps her mother would find something for her to do.

"I've finished my roaming," Belinda informed Marty. "I'm ready to be of some use now."

Marty smiled indulgently at her youngest. "Have things changed?"

Belinda hesitated. How could she express her feelings? To Marty everything must seem exactly the same.

"Things?" queried Belinda almost sadly as she washed her soiled hands at the big basin. "No, not things. Just—just us. People. We change. We've all changed, haven't we, Mama?"

Perhaps Marty did understand. Her eyes misted briefly with tears. She did not allow them to spill. She nodded solemnly at her daughter and Belinda could see that she too was remembering.

"Yeah," she agreed in little more than a whisper. "Yeah, we change. Life is full of change. Seems only yesterday thet I— thet I first entered thet there little log house over there—the one where we first lived—where Clare an' Kate used to live. Ain't no one lives there anymore. First yer pa built us this fine house, an' then Clare built the house yonder fer Kate. Now the little house jest sits there—empty and cold—an'—an' some days—" Marty hesitated until she had her voice more under control. "Some days," she finally went on, "I think I know jest what that little house is feelin'."

Belinda was ready to cry. She hadn't thought about how her mother felt. Hadn't experienced the pain of watching a houseful of children leave one by one. She thought she understood better now.

"But life is like thet," Marty acknowledged, squaring her shoulders. "One mustn't stay pinin' fer the past. Thet don't change a thing. One must be thankful fer what the present offers—what the future can promise."

Marty lifted a corner of her apron to dab at her eyes. When

she looked back at Belinda she was smiling.

"My," she said, "I wouldn't want a one of 'em any different than they turned out to be. Independent! Responsible! Grown-up! I look at folks 'round me, an' I think how blessed I've been. All good children, with keen minds and sturdy bodies. Thet's a powerful lot to be thankin' God fer."

Belinda knew that Marty meant the words with all her heart. She nodded in understanding.

"Let's have us some tea," Marty hastened on. "I'll git it ready whilst ya call Kate. She gits lonesome, Kate does. She still misses her Amy Jo." Marty shrugged resignedly. "But she always will," she admitted. "Thet kind of lonesomeness never goes away."

Belinda left the kitchen. She did not hurry on her way to fetch Kate. She was looking at things—at life—far differently than she had ever done before.

She had never considered lonesomeness as something universal. She had never supposed it to be anything other than temporary and something to be resisted. In her innocence, it should be, and could be, easily disposed of. Fixed up. Remedied. And now her mother was calmly, though with open painfulness, admitting that lonesomeness was an unavoidable part of life.

When one loved, one was vulnerable. There was no guarantee that things would remain constant. Older folks died. Youngsters grew up. Children chose lives of their own. Nothing stayed the same for long.

It was a troubling thought to Belinda. Wasn't there some way—any way—that a person could hang on to what was good? Couldn't one have some control of tomorrow?

But she already knew the answer to that. Would Missie and Ellie be living out West if Marty could have held on to them without at least partially destroying them? Would Amy Jo be miles away from home if Kate could have kept her and given her freedom to grow at the same time? One could not control life, it seemed. Particularly the lives of those you loved. To love was to give freedom. To give freedom often meant pain.

Then why even have a family? Belinda asked herself. *Why let yourself love? Maybe without intending to I've chosen a wiser way. If I never love, never marry, never have children, I won't have to face what Mama—or Kate—is facing now. Is that the answer? Perhaps! Perhaps it is!*

For a moment Belinda felt satisfied. She had solved one of life's riddles for herself.

And then another thought came. *But I already love—it's too late. I was born loving, I guess—or I was taught to love awfully early. I love deeply. Pa—Ma—each of the family. Aunt Virgie. Even Windsor and Potter and the household staff, in a special way. I'm not safe. Not even now. There is no way that anyone can be safe. Not ever. Not as long as you love anyone—anyone at all.*

And Belinda knew better than to assume that life would be better with no one—not one soul—to love.

I guess it's like Mama says, she admitted at last. *One just has to let go of the past, enjoy the present and look forward to whatever the future holds.*

She lifted her face heavenward. "But, oh my, God," she said in a whisper. "Sometimes that's hard. Awfully hard."

A few days later Belinda decided to make a visit to the little log house. She asked Marty about it. After all, it had belonged to Clare and Kate long after it had been Marty's home. They might still feel some ownership and not be comfortable with others snooping about. Belinda didn't want to intrude.

"Go ahead," responded Marty.

"You don't think Kate would mind?"

"Mind? Why no. I think thet she's as happy to be in a new home as I was."

"But I don't want—" began Belinda.

"She's moved everything out," Marty assured her. "The house is totally bare now. S'pose it would be wise to tear it down—but there it still stands."

"Why—why—?" began Belinda, but she didn't finish the question. She couldn't imagine the farmyard without the old house.

But Marty misunderstood, and instead of answering why

the house would never be torn down, she tried to explain instead why it was still standing.

Marty shrugged. "I dunno," she admitted. "Maybe yer pa an' me are jest sentimental. I dunno. We keep sayin' things like, 'Dan might want it,' and stuff like thet. We even talk about makin' it into somethin' else—a granary or a chicken coop—but we won't. I think we both know thet." Marty chuckled, amused by the little game they continued to play between them.

"Well, I need a key. Is it locked?" Belinda asked.

"Oh my, no. Don't s'pose it's ever been locked. Don't know if we even could—'less one put on a padlock of some sort."

Belinda walked down the short trail that led to what used to be Amy Jo's house, feet dragging. She wasn't sure if it was really wise to go there. But she felt she had to—really must do it—if she was to lay the past to rest.

The door opened slowly, creaking its complaint on rusty hinges. Belinda pushed harder and managed to squeeze herself through the small opening that she forced from the tight-sticking door.

The back entry had the same brown walls, the same square in the middle of the floor that opened up to the dumb waiter into the cellar. More than once she and Amy Jo had been scolded for playing with the ropes.

Belinda stood and looked around. The room seemed very small—and bare. There were no coats on coat hooks. No boots in the corner. No pail of slop for the pigs. No life here at all.

Belinda shivered slightly and moved on.

Belinda could not believe her eyes. The kitchen looked as if it belonged in a doll house. She had always thought it—well, at least adequate if not big, but now it looked so small and simple. Much too simple for a woman to really live with each day. The colors were still the same. There was an outdated calendar on the wall, a picture of a little boy holding a brown, curly puppy on the front. Belinda guessed that Kate had not had the heart to discard the picture when the year ended. The last sheet with its month had been discarded.

Belinda crossed into the room that had been used by the family. Memories flooded her mind as she looked about the small area. Here she and Amy Jo had flopped on the floor, lying on their tummies, to draw. Here they had stretched out before the open fire to eat popcorn and giggle over boys. They had rocked in the big rocker that had sat right over there. They had bundled up baby dolls and propped them against the mantel.

She didn't bother with the bedroom Clare and Kate had shared, and she didn't check the room the boys had used. Instead, she passed directly to the room that had been Amy Jo's. It had always been a pale green and yellow—until Amy Jo herself had decided to change that. Amy Jo had wanted a room that was "vibrant." She had been given her way, and "vibrant" her room had become.

Belinda would have been terribly disappointed if the room had been changed—but except for being unfurnished, it was the same. For a minute Belinda stood stock-still, the memories flooding over her and giving her goose bumps. Then she shut her eyes and pictured again the room as she had last seen it. The bed—right there. Against that wall, the dresser with Amy Jo's socks and undies. Amy Jo's nightie always hanging from the peg in the corner. The little desk where she sat to do her drawing. The dolls, the books, the paints and pencils. Belinda could see it all as vividly as if it were actually before her.

And then she opened her eyes slowly. The empty room stared back at her, the marks on the floor where the bed castors had rolled. The smokey-blue paper with its small violet flowers and green leaves was marked here and there by a tack or a smudge. There was a rubbed spot where the desk had stood. Amy Jo had spent so many hours at that desk that she must have soiled the paper. Perhaps Kate had even needed to wipe it with a damp cloth on more than one occasion.

Belinda looked again at the room. In her mind she could hear the childish voice of her then-constant companion. "Oh, Lindy!" Amy Jo would exclaim in exasperation, and Belinda smiled. They were so different, but so close.

With a shiver Belinda turned from the room. Memories were not always pleasant, she decided. Memories could bring pain, too.

She retraced her steps without looking back and slipped

through the door into the afternoon sunshine. The shiver passed up her spine again. She felt that she had suffered a chill. She tugged the complaining heavy wooden door tightly closed behind her.

On the path to the white house Belinda's thoughts were delivering a sharp message. *Nothing is the same. The place, the family—nothing! I am not the same. I love my family—but I don't fit here anymore.*

You don't fit. You don't fit, her shoes seemed to scream with each step that Belinda took along the path back to the big house. She had a hard time to keep from running.

Chapter 9

Return to Boston

The days went far too quickly for Marty, but they dragged somewhat for Belinda. Each morning as she climbed from her bed, she was reminded that she was no longer the young girl who had occupied the room where she now slept. No longer did she fit in with the farmhouse, the out-dated clothes in the closet, the hens and horses. Boston had changed all of that. *At least,* Belinda reasoned, *it must have been Boston.*

There was only one place where she felt she still fit. The little country church—for though the people dressed plainly, the warmth and the preaching tugged at her heart. She had longed for such messages, had ached to be part of such worshipful services. She had sometimes sensed deeply within herself that something important seemed to be missing in the big stone church in Boston.

Yes, in the little country church Belinda felt at home—all in one piece. Whole and complete. But one could not take refuge in the church all week long.

For Belinda, the family devotional time was an extension of the Sunday worship service. She felt mentally and spiritually restored and nourished during the time spent with her mother and father as they read from the Word, discussed thoroughly each scripture passage and spent unhurried time together in prayer.

This is what I've missed the most, Belinda recognized. *The spiritual feeding. The sharing. It's hard to grow if a person is not nourished.*

Belinda decided to make each day at home a source of spiritual refreshment. Often the morning hours slipped by while they sat and talked and prayed.

"I knew that I was missing—what does one call it—'fellowship'? These talking and sharing times," said Belinda one morning as she sat with her mother and father after their devotional time, "but I hadn't realized just how much."

"Don't ya have anyone to talk to?" asked Marty.

"Well, not about—about spiritual things. Not really talk."

"What 'bout yer church?" asked Clark. "Does yer preacher give the Gospel?"

"Well . . . yes and . . . and no," faltered Belinda.

Clark and Marty both looked questioningly at their daughter.

"He—he preaches that Christ is the Son of God," went on Belinda. "And he preaches that Christ came to bring salvation to man. He even talks about our sin and that we need to turn away from it—to repent of our sinful deeds. He uses all the words. Repentance. Redemption. Salvation."

Clark nodded, pleased at Belinda's report.

"But he never really tells people how to find that forgiveness or claim that salvation," Belinda went on. "Sometimes I just get so frustrated, wishing that he'd go that one step further— that he'd tell folks to ask God for His forgiveness—to ask Christ to come into their lives and take over. Trying to be good—all on one's own—just doesn't work."

Clark nodded solemnly. "Does he encourage folks to read the Scriptures for themselves?" he asked.

"No—no, I don't think I've ever heard him suggest it."

Clark was shaking his head, his eyes full of concern. "Thet's a shame," he said soberly. "If folks was readin' the Word, they might discover on their own how to find salvation."

"That's why I worry about Aunt Virgie," went on Belinda. "I'm afraid she just doesn't understand that she has to make a decision herself—a commitment."

"We'll pray along with ya," put in Marty. "We've already been a'prayin', but now thet we know how things be, we'll do it even harder."

Belinda nodded, appreciating the concern of her parents. She was glad they would join with her in her prayer concern.

Many things began to crowd into her visit at home. Belinda spent some time with Luke and Abbie, with Arnie and Anne, with Clare and Kate, and she enjoyed catching up on the happenings of each family. She and Marty hitched the team and drove to Nandry's, Belinda's foster sister. Nandry and Josh were alone now too. All their children had homes of their own, and Nandry boasted proudly about their seven grandchildren.

Belinda was also brought up-to-date on Clae and Joe. They had never come home to the little town they had left so many years before—though they had always intended to. And now Belinda felt that she knew the reason. Clae and her pastor husband Joe would fit in here no better than she herself did.

Belinda heard all the news of Willie and Missie, Lane and Ellie and their families in the West. She was especially anxious for every scrap of information she could gather about Amy Jo and Melissa. Without consciously realizing it, she found herself expecting that the two girls would still be there at the farm, now that she was home.

Belinda ached to just flop across her bed, as was their fashion of old, and talk and talk with her two nieces.

Belinda took a few short rides through the familiar countryside on Copper. He proved to be just as self-willed as ever. Belinda never dared dismount to try to tie him up while she investigated a bush or patch of flowers. She knew how skillful Copper was at leaving for home without her. She did enjoy her outings, regardless, and always returned home with flushed cheeks and shining eyes.

One fall day when the wind was rattling the tree limbs and sending showers of autumn leaves scurrying to the ground, Luke turned his team into the farm lane.

"You busy?" he asked Belinda.

78

"Why, no," she answered, and Marty swung around to question her son with probing eyes.

"I'm not kidnapping her, Ma," teased Luke. "Just wondered if she'd like to make a call with me."

A house call might be good for Belinda, Marty admitted to herself. She had sensed the restlessness in her youngest. Perhaps she was bored. *A call might be just the thing,* Marty reasoned. *Besides, if Luke should need her—if Belinda would feel—would feel a desire to take up her country nursing duties—she might—well, she just might change her mind about going back to Boston.*

Marty nodded encouragingly and Belinda reached for a warm shawl.

"Is it cold?" she asked.

"It's a bit chilly," Luke responded. "I think you'd be wise to take your coat."

Belinda went for her coat and soon joined Luke in the buggy.

"Do you still make a lot of house calls?" she asked him.

"Not like I used to before Jackson came, but yes, I still make my share of them."

"Where are we going today?" asked Belinda.

"Little Becky Winslow has a bad throat. Her mama wants it checked. Didn't want her in my office in case it was contagious," Luke explained.

"I hope it's nothing serious," Belinda commented.

"Doesn't sound like it is, but one always needs to be careful," Luke replied.

They rode in silence for a time; then Luke spoke again. "Well, it's official. Dr. Jackson Brown and Nurse Flo have announced their coming marriage."

"How nice for both of them!" Belinda exclaimed with a smile. She had seen Jackson on one occasion since she had been home. To her relief it had not proved awkward. They had chatted sociably, easily, as two old friends. Belinda was truly happy for Jackson.

"How soon?" Belinda asked.

"Next spring. May. So I won't be losing my nurse immediately. Still, we are training another woman to help in the office.

We don't want to be left with no one in an emergency. We had decided long ago that we should have at least two ladies who know the procedures at all times."

Belinda nodded her agreement.

"Remember that place?" Luke pointed with a finger. Belinda recognized the Coffin farm. The one that Josh had rented to the Simpsons.

"Pa said that Mr. Simpson passed away," Belinda said, her mind churning with many other thoughts.

"He did. It was sudden—and unexpected. By the time Jackson got there, it was too late."

"That's too bad," Belinda commented soberly.

"Mrs. Simpson and Sid still live there," Luke went on.

"That's what Pa said. Looks like they've fixed things up quite a bit," Belinda noted.

"They have. Mr. Simpson worked awfully hard to get it back to what it once was. Say what you like about the family—they can't be accused of being lazy. Hard workers, every one of them."

Belinda kept her thoughts to herself for a few minutes as the team traveled on down the road, leaving the Simpson home behind.

"You mentioned Jackson," she said at last. "Jackson was called when Mr. Simpson died. Does that mean they still haven't forgiven you?"

"Oh, no. I've been there several times. I just was out on another call when it happened, that's all. Why, Drew himself was in to see me awhile back. He was here to visit his ma."

Belinda nodded. "Pa told me," she admitted.

There was silence again. Belinda finally broke it. She wasn't sure what to ask—*how* to ask—but she did want some answers to all her questions.

"Was Drew—has he—has he changed much?"

Luke shook his head and clucked to the team. "Well, yes— and no," he answered. "He's grown-up—filled out—gotten to be a good-looking man."

Nothing different about that, thought Belinda to herself. He was always good-looking.

"He's—he's very mature," Luke continued. "He'll make a

good lawyer. A real good lawyer. Just wish we had him here."

"He doesn't plan to—to come back?"

"I don't expect so. Guess he really didn't say one way or the other—but he did say that he's happy where he is. He's working in a good firm. Getting lots of good experience—making good money too, I'd expect. Not much to come back here for."

Belinda nodded.

"He asked about you," Luke surprised Belinda by saying.

Belinda's eyes widened. "He did?"

"Said he never did thank you—properly—for your part in his surgery."

Belinda's eyes darkened with the memory. It had been one of the most difficult experiences of her life.

"What did you tell him?" asked Belinda.

"Just said that an elderly lady had been brought from the train to us and that you'd gone off to the city to become her private nurse. He seemed happy for you."

A few more minutes of silence slipped by.

"Luke," asked Belinda slowly, "do you think the city is where I really belong?"

The question was put so seriously that Luke could sense the depth of feeling Belinda had as she asked.

"That's a question only you can answer," he responded kindly, and Belinda nodded her head.

"It's just—just—I don't know anymore," she admitted. "I—I don't seem to fit here."

"What is 'fitting'?" Luke asked. "How does one feel when one 'fits'?"

"Well, I—I—like I used to feel, I guess," Belinda stammered. "I never used to even think about fitting before."

Luke nodded. "When I'd been away—to get my training," he said slowly, "and came home again—well, I wasn't quite sure if this was the place for me or not. I sure didn't fit in the same groove that I'd been in before, but I decided that there was little use looking back. That really wasn't where I wanted to be any-way—a young squirt tagging along after Doc. So it seemed like the only thing to do was to make myself a new groove. One of my very own. And I set to work doing that. I feel quite comfortable in my little spot now—and Abbie and the kids, they seem happy, too."

"I guess that's what I'm going to have to do," agreed Belinda, and she thought of Boston. She didn't really look forward to settling permanently in the big city, but to her thinking there was really nothing else that she could do—at least for now. Aunt Virgie needed her—and she certainly didn't seem to have a place here in the country anymore.

She sighed deeply. Life could be so complicated.

"Hey," Luke said, reaching across to squeeze her folded hands. "I have faith in you. You'll know the right thing to do when the time comes."

"But—" began Belinda. "I—I can't just put it off forever—and—and drift. I have to make up my mind sooner or later."

"And you will," said Luke. "I'm counting on it."

They had reached their destination. Luke hopped down and turned to help Belinda, then tied the team and lifted his black bag from the buggy.

"Let's take a look at Becky's throat," he said to Belinda and they entered the house together.

It turned out to be simple tonsillitis, and Luke left some medicine and soon they were on their way again.

"It's always a relief when it isn't something serious," Luke said and Belinda nodded in agreement. *If only life could always be so simple and straightforward,* she thought.

Marty asked Belinda if there were any neighbors she wished to visit. Belinda pondered for a few minutes. All her school chums were married women, and a number of them had moved from the area. She shook her head slowly. "Only Ma Graham, I guess. I don't really know who else is still around."

And so Belinda and Marty hitched the team again and started to the Grahams.

"It's been awhile since I've been over to Ma Graham's myself," Marty confessed. "I keep tellin' myself thet I must git goin', but then somethin' more comes up thet needs doin' and I put it off agin."

Marty had been "doin" all the time Belinda had been home.

The garden produce had to be brought in and put in the root cellar, and the apples had to be picked and stored and the kraut had to be made—and on and on it went. Her hands were always busy, yet she had not allowed Belinda much opportunity to help.

"Now, you don't want to go back to Boston with yer hands all stained an' rough," she would scold mildly. "You jest sit there an' talk whilst I work."

Belinda had not cared for the arrangement and she had usually found some tasks, such as churning butter or mixing up a cake, while the two of them shared the kitchen.

But now it was visiting day. Marty seemed to look forward to the break.

"Ma's been a mite poorly," she informed Belinda.

Belinda, concerned, asked what the problem was.

"Luke says it's jest old age, plain an' simple. She's had a busy life—a hard life, Ma has, an' I guess thet one can't help it when it shows. She blames it all on her gallbladder," went on Marty.

"Has she thought of having surgery?" asked Belinda.

"Well, to do thet, she'd hafta go to the hospital over to the city, an' Ma don't want to do thet. Says she'd rather jest put up with it."

"That might not be a good idea," Belinda continued.

"Well, wise or not, thet's the way us old folks think sometimes," said Marty, putting herself in the same age group as Ma Graham.

They were welcomed with love and enthusiasm by the older woman. "Belinda, let me look at ya!" she cried. "My don't ya look nice. So grown-up and pretty. My, how the years have flown. Seems jest yesterday ya was here delivering me another granddaughter."

Belinda remembered. It had been the first delivery Luke had allowed her to help with.

And it was on my way home that Drew stopped me, she silently remembered, and felt her cheeks flush slightly.

Like Ma said, it had been a long time ago.

"An' you, Marty," Ma teased. "Seems it's been almost thet long since I've seen even you."

Marty laughed and the two women embraced.

Tea was soon ready and the three sat down for a good chat. Time passed quickly as Belinda caught up on each member of the Graham family. Ma even had some great-grandchildren. She beamed as she spoke of them.

All too soon it was time to go. Marty left with the promise that she wouldn't wait so long to be back again, and Ma promised to have one of her boys drive her over to the Davis farm one day soon.

"Thet was a good idea, to visit Ma," Marty said to Belinda on the way home. "I'm so glad thet ya thought of it. Ma always did hold you as somethin' special."

"I've missed her at church," Belinda said. "It seemed strange not to see her there."

"Well, it's her bad leg thet keeps her from church," Mary informed her daughter. "Ya notice how she can't take a step without thet cane—an' she can't climb steps at all anymore."

Belinda had noticed, and it bothered her. It was just one more thing that was changing—and she felt helpless to do anything about it.

Eventually the day came for Belinda to return to Boston. It was cold and windy, and Belinda shivered as she pulled on her light traveling coat. She realized that she should have brought something warmer. The weather had been so much milder when she had left Boston that she hadn't thought of what it might be six weeks later.

Her simple country frocks had all been hung back in the closet. Belinda noticed Marty's eyes lingering on them there.

Belinda commented carelessly, "Who knows when I might be back again?" But she couldn't help but wonder if Marty thought, just as she did, that those dresses might never be worn by Belinda again.

"Ya better wrap this heavy shawl around yer shoulders," Marty said, handing one to her, and Belinda did not protest.

The trip into town was a quiet one. They seemed to have said everything there was to say. Now, the thought of the separation ahead made talking difficult.

"Yer sure you'll be warm enough?" Marty asked anxiously as Belinda returned the shawl.

"It's plenty warm on the train," Belinda assured her.

"Ya won't need to git off?"

"Not until I get to Boston."

"Do they know when to expect ya?"

"I left the schedule with Windsor," responded Belinda. "He'll be there with the carriage to meet me. He is most dependable, Windsor is."

Marty nodded.

The family was gathered at the station to see her off. Even the youngsters had been allowed to leave school early so they could be on hand for Belinda's departure. There was a great deal of shuffling about and making small talk while they waited for the slow-moving minutes to tick by.

At last they heard the shrill of the whistle in the distance. The train would soon be pulling into the station. Belinda began her round of goodbyes, leaving her ma and pa for last.

She hated goodbyes. The tears, the hugs, the promises. She wished there were an easier way to take one's leave. But it was the doubts that made this goodbye most difficult. Belinda had so many doubts—so many worries. She wondered for the hundredth time if she was doing the right thing. When would she be home again? What would bring her back? Some tragedy? She prayed not. But who could tell? Her mother and father were getting older. Belinda had seen firsthand the aging of Ma Graham. In a few years' time her ma and pa could age like that, she knew.

Belinda shivered at the thought.

"You need a heavier coat," Marty said again.

"I have one in Boston, Mama, and I won't need one until I get there. Really. The train will be nice and warm."

Marty held Belinda close as though to protect her from the chill of the wind and the pain of the world.

"Write," she whispered. "I 'most live fer yer letters."

"I will," promised Belinda.

"An' don't worry—'bout home. We're fine," continued Marty, and Belinda wondered just how much her mother knew about the feelings that churned the girl's insides.

Clark held her then. She felt his arms tighten about her, and for a fleeting moment she was tempted to change her plans. But she knew she had to return to Boston. She kissed her mother one last time and then, amid shouts of "goodbye," she climbed the train steps and selected a seat just as the big engine began to move the cars down the tracks.

Belinda leaned from the window and waved one last time.

The train was taking her back to Boston. *Back to where I belong,* thought Belinda.

But her mind hurried on.

If that is so, she asked herself, *why do I feel so empty inside? Why are my cheeks wet with tears? Why do I feel as if I've just been torn away from everything that is solid?*

Belinda didn't have the answers.

Chapter 10

Back to Normal?

Belinda had arranged her return so she would be back at Marshall Manor the day before Mrs. Stafford-Smyth was due home. This would give her a chance to be settled in and able to give full attention to the older woman upon her arrival.

Dependable Windsor met Belinda at the station just as she had known he would. Belinda thought he seemed almost glad to see her, though he wouldn't have thought it proper to admit as much. Belinda smiled to herself as she settled in among the robes he had brought. The cold wind was blowing in Boston also, and Windsor no doubt had noticed which coat Belinda had worn as she left.

The house looked the same—big, beautiful, and inviting. Belinda tried not to compare it with the little farm home she had just left, but it was difficult not to do so. She was looking forward to having indoor plumbing once again. It would be so nice to soak leisurely in a tub filled with warm water from a faucet. Belinda felt as if she had scarcely had a proper bath since she had left Boston. Taking a bath in a galvanized tub just wasn't the same.

Even the distant and cool Potter seemed pleased to see her and bustled about asking how she could be of service, and what would Miss like for her dinner. Belinda could scarcely believe her eyes and ears.

Windsor insisted on carrying her suitcase and hatbox up

the stairs, and Belinda followed close behind, anxious to see if her room was really as pretty as she remembered it.

She sighed deeply as she looked about her. Everything was just as she had pictured it. She motioned to Windsor to set her suitcase by the bureau and excused him with a simple "Thank you."

She was anxious to have a nice, sudsy soak. Even as she thought about it, she could hear water running and crossed the room to find Ella already in the bathroom.

"I thought you might like a nice bath, miss," Ella explained and Belinda gratefully assured her that she would.

"You just hop right in, miss," Ella said on her way out of the bathroom, "and I'll unpack for you. What do you wish me to lay out for dinner, miss?"

Have I really lived like this? Belinda asked herself. And then, *Yes. I'd quite forgotten. Before I left I'd gotten used to being treated like a—a spoiled, pampered lady of leisure.*

"Something simple," she smiled at the maid, "seeing as I will be dining alone. I really am very tired and feel the need for my bed far more than the need for food."

"Of course, miss," answered Ella.

"You pick something," Belinda called over her shoulder as she headed for the tubful of warm water.

It was delightful to lower herself into the warmth and the suds and let the water soak away the fatigue from her back and shoulders. Belinda would have lingered longer had not Ella called to her.

"I've finished the unpacking, miss, and laid out your gown. Cook said she will serve in half an hour. Do you wish me to do your hair?"

Belinda considered the offer. It would feel good to have Ella do her hair again. It seemed so long since she'd had it done properly. But she was weary—and she had little time. She called back, "No thank you. I'll need to hurry. I'll just pin it up for tonight."

"Very well, miss," said Ella and Belinda heard the door close.

She climbed from the tub and dried on the large, fluffy towel, noticing how soft and white it was.

Perhaps it has been good for me to be away, she reasoned. *I'll take more notice of things that I've been taking for granted.*

Belinda hurried, remembering that Potter did not suffer tardiness with pleasure.

She was almost breathless as she entered the dining room. It seemed so strange to sit down to a table all by herself. Especially when she had just come from a family where several plates usually crowded the table.

Homesickness tugged at Belinda's heart as she seated herself and bowed her head to say grace while Windsor stood by waiting to serve her.

The dinner looked delicious, and Belinda might have enjoyed it more had she been less tired—and less lonely. Out of habit she forked the food to her mouth but hardly tasted a thing. After she had done some sort of justice to what had been prepared, she excused herself and announced that she was retiring for the night.

With no early-rising roosters or bellowing cows to awaken her, Belinda slept late the next morning. When she finally did open her eyes and study her clock, she was shocked to see that it was quarter of ten. She threw back her covers and rang for Ella.

Ella responded immediately and Belinda stopped brushing her hair long enough to say, "Run my bath, would you, please, Ella? I've overslept. Mrs. Stafford-Smyth is due in at twelve-thirty."

Ella nodded. "Windsor has been fretting," she acknowledged.

"Why didn't someone awaken me?"

"We all knew you were tired, miss. Potter said to let you be."

"Potter?" Belinda's eyebrows went up and then she smiled. There had been a time when Potter would have taken delight in seeing her summoned from her bed.

"Cook said to let her know when you were ready for breakfast," declared Ella, coming from the bathroom where the tub was steaming.

"No breakfast. I don't have time," Belinda told her. "Tell Cook I'm really not that hungry."

Ella looked troubled. "She'll insist on some fresh juice at least, miss," Ella dared forecast.

"Some juice then. Up here. And perhaps a scone. That's all."

Ella left and Belinda bustled about. This time she did not linger in the tub.

At the time previously set by Windsor, Belinda was in the front hall, her hat on straight, her heavy coat buttoned properly. She was ready to meet the train.

Belinda felt a surge of excitement as the wheels of the carriage bumped along the cobblestone road. It seemed a very long time since she had seen Mrs. Stafford-Smyth. She was looking forward to sharing the news from her hometown. *Well, at least some of the news,* Belinda reasoned. She knew she wouldn't share with the older woman some of the thoughts and feelings she'd had while away.

In fact, the more Belinda thought about it, the more she wondered just what she would be able to share. Her trip home had been so—so personal—so troubling. Maybe she wouldn't dare discuss much of it at all.

But she would ask Mrs. Stafford-Smyth to tell her all about her holiday in New York. There certainly would be plenty for them to talk about. She'd hear all about the plays, the concerts, the dress shops. They would talk about all the things Mrs. Stafford-Smyth had experienced—but they would not discuss the conflicting emotions Belinda had battled, she decided.

The train arrived on time, and Belinda held her coat securely about her and scanned the crowd for Mrs. Stafford-Smyth. Windsor spotted her first. "There's M'lady!" he exclaimed, and even the proper Windsor could not keep the excited tremor from his voice.

Belinda saw her then and ran to meet her.

"Oh, my deah, my deah!" cried the older woman, "how I have missed you."

There were tears in Mrs. Stafford-Smyth's eyes as she held the girl. If Belinda had doubted the reason why she was back in Boston, she understood and accepted it thoroughly now. *She needs me.* She really had no one else. A houseful of servants was not family, even though Mrs. Stafford-Smyth cared for each of them.

Windsor hastened the two of them into the carriage, declaring that he would return later for the luggage.

"And how was *your* trip, deah?" asked the older woman.

"Fine," replied Belinda. "I was able to see everyone—well, everyone who still lives at home."

"That's nice," smiled the lady. But in spite of the smile, Belinda worried about the tiredness in Mrs. Stafford-Smyth's face.

"Have you not been feeling well?" Belinda asked.

Mrs. Stafford-Smyth waved the question aside. "I've been fine," she maintained, "just fine."

Belinda did not press her further. "And how was your trip?" she said instead. "I am so anxious to hear all about it. It must have been terribly exciting."

The older woman looked at her evenly. "Not really," she replied at last.

Belinda was surprised. *Maybe Mrs. Stafford-Smyth's trip has not gone well.* "You aren't telling me something," Belinda said softly. "What is it? Were you sick while you were away?"

Mrs. Stafford-Smyth shook her head, and then tears began to form and to run down her face, splashing unheeded into her fur collar. "It's just—just—" she sniffed, "that I couldn't think of anything else but you, deah. I kept thinking you wouldn't come back once you got home again. I lived every day in feah, and didn't feel like doing anything. Celia neahly tossed me out she was so annoyed with me, but I—I just couldn't help it."

Belinda reached out to take her employer's hand, giving her a handkerchief. "That's all right," she comforted. "I'm here. I came back just as I said I would."

"I'm so glad. So glad," breathed the older woman. "Now things can get back to normal again."

Normal? thought Belinda. She had just moved back and forth between two very different worlds. *What,* she wondered, *is normal?*

But things did fall back into a daily routine. The two women picked up where they had left off, sharing their meals, their handwork, their lives. Little by little they spoke about some of the experiences of their time apart, too. It seemed that the one had been as miserable as the other—but for quite different reasons.

The windy fall days turned to winter chill, and snow began to pile up on Thomas's flower beds. This time there was no discussion of a trip abroad to avoid the winter. They knew without saying so that they both had consented to suffer it through. Belinda realized that she was already looking forward to spring even as she saw the winds tuck the flowers away for the winter.

Belinda kept her promise to her mother. Each week she wrote a lengthy letter home and looked forward to the reply that was sure to come. She shared the letters with Mrs. Stafford-Smyth, who seemed to enjoy them almost as much as Belinda did.

When Christmas came, they celebrated with strangers again. In its own way, it was a joyous time. Mrs. Stafford-Smyth had enjoyed planning the holiday event and having the festive table surrounded by dinner guests. Their guests, too, appreciated the time spent in the big house with the kind woman and her staff.

But for Belinda the most special moments occurred each day as the two of them spent time together studying the Bible. Since her trip to New York, Mrs. Stafford-Smyth seemed much more sensitive and open to spiritual things. Belinda wondered if something particular had happened there.

But her employer never said anything about such an event. Belinda held her tongue, but continued to wonder—and to pray.

Chapter 11

An Exciting Happening

Belinda knew that her folks at home were praying for Mrs. Stafford-Smyth as well. Each morning as the two studied a Bible lesson together, Belinda watched closely for any flickers of understanding on the part of the older woman.

Mrs. Stafford-Smyth did listen attentively. She also attended church services regularly. But Belinda could not help but feel that the woman did not really understand the true significance of the Christian faith. Mrs. Stafford-Smyth seemed to feel that if one tried to be good—was more good than evil—then hopefully God's scales would tip in the person's favor.

Belinda selected scriptures dealing with the sacrificial death of the Savior, the need for a personal faith, the glorious hope of heaven because of what Christ Jesus had done on the sinner's behalf. But though the woman looked sincere, each Bible lesson seemed to fall on deaf ears. Belinda thought often of Christ's parable of the seed and the sower. She wondered if Mrs. Stafford-Smyth would ever choose to be "good ground" or if the evil one would always "snatch the seed" away before it had a chance to root—to grow.

Belinda prayed more earnestly and searched more diligently for appropriate scriptures.

One Sunday morning as Easter approached, Belinda left the morning worship feeling dry and empty. The sermon, though it had referred to the Cross and what it meant for sinful mankind, seemed so dry and lifeless. It left much to be desired, in Belinda's thinking.

If he only had gone on—told the rest of the story—explained the meaning of it all, Belinda chaffed. *But no. He stopped right there—short, leaving his congregation to sort through the whole thing for themselves. No wonder they cannot seem to understand the meaning of the Cross.*

Belinda felt like crying as she climbed into the carriage with her employer for the ride home.

"Wasn't that a wonderful sermon, deah?" asked Mrs. Stafford-Smyth as soon as she had properly arranged her skirts.

Belinda's head came up. There was something unusual in the woman's tone. To Belinda's surprise the lady's face was shining in a way that Belinda had never seen before. Belinda could not speak. She just nodded dumbly.

"I've heard it ovah and ovah," the older lady went on with reverent enthusiasm; "but you know—I've nevah really understood the meaning of it befoah. This mawnin' as I listened, it all came to me just like that. Imagine! The Son of God himself dyin' in the place of *me.* Isn't it *glorious?* Just glorious! Why, I bowed my head right there where I sat and just thanked Him ovah and ovah. I nearly had one of those—what do they call it?—revival meetings all by myself."

Belinda stared in wonder. Mrs. Stafford-Smyth had gotten what her pastor at home would call "a good dose of old-fashioned religion"—and in the most unlikely place too. In her cold, formal city church.

"Oh, Aunt Virgie!" Belinda cried, throwing her arms around the older woman. She wanted to say, *That's what I've tried so hard to show you. That's what I've been praying for, working for,* but that seemed irrelevant. The wonderful thing was that Mrs. Stafford-Smyth now knew the truth for herself. *I can hardly wait to write home with the good news!* she exulted. She knew that her folks would be almost as excited as she was.

"You know," the woman went on, her face still shining, "all those readings that we've been doing together? Do you remembah where you found them? I'd like us to read them all again—now that I think I understand what they'ah really saying. Could we?"

"Why, of course," Belinda was thrilled to agree.

"I can hardly wait to tell Windsah—and Pottah. I'll bet they don't understand it eithah. Cook might—there's a feeling I have about Cook. But the girls—I doubt if eithah of them do. Do you think they do?"

Belinda hadn't gone that far in her thinking. She was a bit chagrined as she thought of the other household members. She had been concentrating all of her time and prayers on Mrs. Stafford-Smyth.

"You know, we should have the whole staff gathah for the Bible-reading times," Mrs. Stafford-Smyth continued. "My, I'd just hate it terribly if any one of them right in my own house missed knowing the truth."

Belinda could not believe her ears, but Mrs. Stafford-Smyth was still not finished.

"That's what we'll do. Right aftah breakfast each mawnin'. We'll all meet togethah in the north parlawh. You can choose the reading and then we'll talk about it."

Belinda had a momentary qualm at the thought of leading the whole household in the morning Bible lesson. *What if someone asks a difficult question?* she thought. *I'm sure no theologian. It wouldn't be at all difficult for one of them to stump me—badly.*

But she nodded her head in agreement. Maybe now Mrs. Stafford-Smyth would be able to help her explain some of the scriptural truths.

It was later that evening that Belinda was able to ask the question that had been gnawing at her all day. Seated in the cozy little parlor having tea and biscuits before retiring, Mrs. Stafford-Smyth was still bubbling with her earlier experience. Belinda listened joyfully and then when the lady paused, Belinda posed her question.

"What was it that made you see it—understand the truth of salvation—all of a sudden?"

Mrs. Stafford-Smyth stopped, teacup raised almost to her lips, and thought about the question. Then she answered assuredly, simply, "Why, I suppose it was the Holy Spirit. Just like the Scripture tells us, 'He will teach you all things.' I couldn't 'see' it on my own. My spiritual eyesight was 'darkened.' I don't think I wanted to know the truth. I shut it out without realizing it, just like the Scripture says. I wanted to manage on my own. I had to reach the place where I was willing to hear the truth."

Belinda could only stare.

"You read those verses the othah mawnin'," the older lady told her. "Remembah? Of course at the time they didn't mean a thing to me—but I understand them now."

"Of course," said Belinda.

That night as Belinda knelt beside her bed she had something new to pray about—to rejoice over. But she had a confession, too.

"Dear Father," she prayed, "forgive me for feeling that I had to 'convert' Aunt Virgie when it was your business all the time. I know that we Christians are to share our faith—help me to be faithful in doing that. But, Lord, never let me believe it is my doing when someone reaches out to you. It is only through the work of your Holy Spirit that any lost person can be drawn to you, the Father. Aunt Virgie accepted the sacrifice of Christ only because your Spirit helped her to understand it. Thank you, Lord, for showing her. Thank you that she was able to understand and accept it. And now help the two of us as we try to share this Good News with the staff. And remind me— always—that my task is just to share. Yours is to do the converting."

The whole household soon felt the effects of the conversion of their "Lady." Mrs. Stafford-Smyth was open about what had happened. She did not force the issue with others, but she let it be known that she expected her staff to be in attendance at the Bible readings.

She had Belinda read, gave opportunity for discussion, but pressured no one to accept or refute the truths.

"God will do that through His Spirit," she kept reminding Belinda. "He is the only One who knows the innah parts of the soul." But Mrs. Stafford-Smyth did not lightly regard her Christian duty. She and Belinda spent much time in prayer each day for everyone sharing in the morning study.

Then Mrs. Stafford-Smyth extended her mission to share the Good News.

"We need to have anothah dinnah party," she informed Belinda. "I don't know if any of my old friends really understand the truth. I believe they think much like I did; that one gives God proper respect and tries to do good toward his fellowman, and, in return, the Lord blinks while the person squeezes through the gates."

Belinda smiled.

Mrs. Stafford-Smyth thought for a while. At length she continued. "You know," she said, "I think it's moah than that. I don't think I understood what sin was. I thought sin was killing folks, or stealing from your neighbah, or cheating the poah. And so it is—but it's so much more. I didn't understand that the sin that broke the heart of God and kept one from entering heaven was the sin of rejection—of not acknowledging and accepting Christ's death on Calvary in my place. That is why God would not have been able to let Virginia Stafford-Smyth enter the gates. I hadn't recognized my sin of unacceptance—unbelief, if you will—and accepted what He had done for me on Calvary."

Belinda solemnly nodded again.

"Oh, but it's so wonderful when it is all taken care of," continued the older woman, tears forming in her eyes. And then she hastened on. "Well, we need that dinnah party, that's foah sure."

Potter, Windsor, and Cook were all summoned and Mrs. Stafford-Smyth discussed her plans. All the old crowd were to be invited, she said, and in some way—some way—the Spirit would reveal to her a way to share her new-found faith. She didn't want to depart this world without telling her dear old friends the truth of the Gospel, she informed the staff members.

The night of the dinner party arrived.

"What do you plan to do?" Belinda asked Mrs. Stafford-Smyth as they waited for their guests to arrive.

"I don't know," she replied honestly. She still had not received her directions from the Lord as to how to go about sharing.

All the guests had been seated at the dining room table, and Windsor was standing ready to serve at a nod from his mistress. She had to say something. She would stall for a bit of time—sort of set the mood—while she waited for an idea from the Lord.

"Belinda and I have established a new"—she hesitated over what word to choose—"habit," she went on. "A good habit. We read togethah before we dine. Belinda, deah, would you bring the Scriptures and read that same portion that we read togethah this mawnin'?"

With a rather pale face, Belinda went to get the Bible. She settled herself nervously in her chair at the table and began to read. At first her voice was low and trembling, but gradually it steadied. Fidgeting stopped. Dinner guests lifted their heads to catch the words.

Belinda read, "For when we were yet without strength, in due time Christ died for the ungodly. For scarcely for a righteous man will one die: yet peradventure for a good man some would even dare to die. But God commendeth his love toward us, in that, while we were yet sinners, Christ died for us."

"Ah, yes," breathed Mrs. Stafford-Smyth as Belinda carefully closed the Book and handed it to Windsor. "Let us pray." The prayer was a thanksgiving for the food that they were to enjoy, but Mrs. Stafford-Smyth also included a thanks for the truth presented in the Scripture reading.

After a few awkward coughs and throat-clearings, the meal was served.

Before the talk around the table had opportunity to stray to other things, Mrs. Stafford-Smyth turned to Mr. Allenby. "How do you understand that Scripture?" she asked simply.

For a moment the dignified man mentally scrambled around for some explanation, his shrewd little wife casting furtive glances about the table.

Mr. Walsh spoke up, "Why, it told of the death of the Son of God for sinners," he stated in a straightforward manner.

"For sinnahs," mused Mrs. Stafford-Smyth. "Who are the sinnahs?" And so began a lively discussion. Belinda could not help but smile at times. Never had this elderly crowd become so involved in animated conversation.

There were differences of opinion of course. Mr. Allenby believed that though all of mankind might "err" on occasion, eventually everyone would be ushered in to enjoy the bliss of an eternal heaven. Mr. Whitley disagreed. Heaven was a state of mind, he argued. Mr. Walsh went so far as to declare that heaven was reserved for a "special" group, but he wasn't sure just who or what determined the special ones.

Mrs. Allenby sat silently, her eyes darting back and forth between the speakers, while Mrs. Whitley fidgeted with her napkin and turned from pale white to blushing red and back again.

Celia Prescott was not going to allow the men of the crowd to have all the say. She broke into the conversation with enthusiasm, making her point and then camouflaging it with a bit of humor. Belinda decided that Celia Prescott did not want to be taken too seriously where religion was concerned.

But gently, and with skillful courtesy, Mrs. Stafford-Smyth managed to steer the conversation in the direction she wished it to take. Eventually there seemed nowhere else for the discussion to go but to some sort of sensible conclusion.

"It seems from what you have said," Mrs. Stafford-Smyth nodded toward Mr. Allenby, pinning him with his own words, "that it isn't possible for anyone to live perfectly. That all of us, in one way or anothah, at one time or anothah—well—sins."

He sputtered a bit, but he finally conceded the point.

Mrs. Stafford-Smyth then turned to Mr. Walsh. "And you think that heaven was made a special place—for those who rightfully belong there."

He chuckled, nodding sociably. Mr. Walsh, with his unique sense of humor, did not seem to be able to take even heaven seriously.

"Well, I have reason to agree," continued the lady. "If heaven were for everyone, as you believe, John," she said, turning to Mr. Whitley, "then it seems to me it wouldn't be one bit bettah than what we already have heah on earth. Soon we would have the killing, the war, the poverty—all the things we have heah. That's not the kind of heaven I would look forward to entering."

Heads nodded solemnly.

"So the only thing left," Mrs. Stafford-Smyth went on, "is the business of how one gets to go there."

Mrs. Whitley fidgeted morosely, her face looking pale again. Mrs. Allenby darted a look at her hostess, then seemed to measure her distance to the door. Belinda wondered if she was going to make a run for it.

The men still seemed perfectly unaware of the direction and intent of the conversation. To them it was a jolly good discussion, with some life—some spirit. They hadn't enjoyed anything quite as much for a long time.

"We make our own heaven," argued Mr. Whitley. "If we are miserly and mean and can't get along with our fellowman, we live and die that way."

"But that's not exactly right," cut in Mr. Allenby. "There has to be something *beyond* life—we all know that in here." He placed his hand over his chest.

"What gives us the right to determine who gets to heaven—and how? We are no different than our neighbor," said Mr. Walsh with a chuckle, feeling that he had scored a good point even though he did not feel too strongly about the matter.

"Exactly!" said Mrs. Stafford-Smyth emphatically, making Mr. Walsh beam even more. "Exactly. We do not have the right to do that."

There were nods around the table, everyone seeming to agree. And then Mrs. Stafford-Smyth folded her napkin carefully, looked evenly at her guests and continued. "Only God has that right. And He tells us exactly how it's to be. We are all sinnahs—every one of us—just like you said, Wilbur. We won't be allowed entrance into heaven," with a nod toward Mr. Walsh, "not in our sinful condition. That is what the crucifixion was all about—Christ, the sinless Son of God, dying in ou-ah place. The only hope we have of heaven is in recognizing and accepting what He has done for us.

"How did that scripture say it, Belinda? 'While we were yet sinnahs, Christ died for us.' It's just as you said, Mr. Walsh. Heaven is for a selected group. Those who believe and accept what Christ has done."

She turned then to Mr. Whitley. "And you were right, too—almost. We do determine our own destiny. We don't make our own heaven or hell, but we do make our own choices that determine which place we will go to. God does not condemn anyone. He has provided heaven for the just—through faith. And hell is for the unjust—the unbelievers. By choosing Christ's salvation or by choosing to go ou-ah own way, we determine which one shall be ou-ah abode."

Those around the table drew a collective breath. The conversation had suddenly gotten rather personal. But Mrs. Stafford-Smyth was still not finished.

"It took me a long time to see that," she admitted. "Fact is, the truth just got home to me a few Sundays ago. I finally saw it—understood it. So I did just as Scripture says. I repented of my sin and I accepted what Christ did for me so long ago. I thanked Him for it and asked Him to help me live the rest of my life as He wants it lived. I was slow—I know. I had heard the message all those yeahs and still didn't properly understand it. I do hope that you all have been much more spiritually wise than I have been. I really don't understand how I could have been so blind—for so long."

Then Mrs. Stafford-Smyth flashed her dinner guests a winning smile. "Still," she said kindly, "it is a truth to be thinking on. Not one of us heah is getting any youngah. It is wise to be sure we're ready for the hereaftah." Then after a pause to allow time for quiet reflection and with a complete change of tone, she said, "Windsah, would you serve the coffee, please?"

Chapter 12

The Bend in the Road

A few days later Mrs. Celia Prescott came to call. She chatted on about the past trip to New York, the new spring fashions, the play at the local theater, but all the time she bubbled and enthused, Belinda had the feeling that the woman had something else on her mind.

"If you'll excuse me," Belinda said when they had finished their tea, "it's such a lovely day, I think I'll take a little walk in the garden." The two ladies nodded and Belinda left. She couldn't have explained why, but she had the impression that Mrs. Prescott might want to talk privately with Mrs. Stafford-Smyth.

Belinda stayed out in the garden talking with old Thomas, enjoying the clear air and bold sunshine until she heard Mrs. Prescott's carriage leave the yard.

When she went in, Mrs. Stafford-Smyth still sat in the chair where Belinda had left her, her open Bible in her lap. At the sound of Belinda's step she lifted her head. "We need to pray," she said simply. "Celia is—is struggling."

"Did she—?" Belinda began, but Mrs. Stafford-Smyth interrupted her.

"She is just like I was—blinded to the truth. She wants so badly to be 'good enough' to get to heaven on her own. To admit that she is a sinnah—well, that puts her on a common level with all mankind—and Celia has nevah thought of herself as common.

"How foolish and proud we are," mourned the elderly lady, tears forming in her eyes. "The creature trying to outwit the Creator. Pretending to be something we know we are not. Why do we do that, Belinda?"

Belinda had no answer.

"Well, we will just keep praying," declared Mrs. Stafford-Smyth. "Who knows what the Spirit might do in the hearts of the ones who listened to His Word the othah night?"

But one result of that dinner-party discussion was completely unexpected—even to Mrs. Stafford-Smyth and Belinda who had been praying. It was loyal, dignified Windsor who responded to the truth of the Scriptures as they had been discussed that evening. The butler had stood patiently and unobtrusively by, serving the dinner guests as they animately discussed the meaning of the Scripture passage.

But the truths that had been presented so simply had touched the heart of the old man, and in the privacy of his own chambers he had turned in faith to the Savior.

Mrs. Stafford-Smyth was overjoyed. Though Windsor did not want to be fussed over regarding his well-thought-out decision, it did cause no small stir in the household.

Windsor summoned Belinda, his face ashen white and his voice choked with emotion. "Come quickly, miss," he trembled. "Something is the matter with M'lady."

Belinda sped from the room. She had been sitting alone waiting for Mrs. Stafford-Smyth to join her for breakfast.

"Call the doctor," she flung over her shoulder as she ran.

A shocked Sarah stood at the bedroom door ringing her hands and sobbing. She had discovered her mistress when she had gone in to help her dress. Belinda rushed past her to reach the older woman. *She could be seriously ill* was Belinda's frantic thought. *She might need immediate attention.*

But as she bent over the woman, it was quickly obvious to Belinda that a doctor would avail nothing. Mrs. Stafford-Smyth was gone. She had passed away sometime during the night—without a struggle, probably without pain.

Belinda stood clasping her hands tightly together, too stunned to cry. *Oh, God,* she prayed silently, *what do we all do now? How will we manage to go on without her?*

She reached down to draw the hands over the older woman's bosom and lift the sheet carefully to cover the face.

"Oh, Aunt Virgie," she said aloud, her voice catching, "I loved you so."

The tears came then, deep sobbing tears. Belinda lowered herself to the floor, leaned her head against the bed and let sorrow consume her.

The doctor and Windsor found her there, her body trembling, her face swollen from crying.

"Come, miss," Windsor said kindly and lifted her to her feet. He led her from the room while the doctor performed whatever duty was required. She allowed herself to be guided downstairs by Windsor's steadying hand.

"Sit here," Windsor said, lowering Belinda to a chair. "I'll fetch some tea." Belinda wanted to protest, but she didn't have the strength. *What does it matter?* she thought distractedly. *I'll sip from the cup if Windsor wants.*

The hush over the house was broken only by a sob now and then as one staff member or another failed to hide his or her grief.

Belinda remembered very little about the rest of the day—the rest of the week. She moved as one in a dream—unfeeling, unnoticing, except for the huge, painful emptiness within her. Over and over she asked herself, "What will we all do now?" But there didn't seem to be any immediate answer.

She phoned LeSouds and ordered appropriate mourning garments delivered. Someone else took care of the funeral arrangements and sent notices to those who should know. Many bouquets were delivered to the door. Belinda watched as they covered the mantel and then the tables in the parlor. They meant nothing to her. *Aunt Virgie is gone* echoed numbly through her mind.

Somehow everyone made it through the awful day of the

funeral. Belinda watched as the coffin was lowered into the ground. Around the grave stood the friends and the staff of Mrs. Stafford-Smyth. Franz and Pierre had sent telegrams and flowers, not having enough travel time to make it to the funeral.

It all was so—so *final* to Belinda. She found it difficult to fathom—to believe that their dear friend was gone. But no one could change the fact.

Back at the house, Belinda laid aside her veiled black hat. She stripped the black gloves from her shaking fingers and turned to Windsor. "Please don't bother with dinner for me," she said through lips stiff with grief. "I'm really not hungry."

He nodded and quietly left.

Silently Belinda climbed the stairs to her room.

Sometime later there was a tap on Belinda's door. She stirred restlessly in her chair by the window. *Who could want me?* she wondered. *And why? Surely no one had the poor judgment to come calling on such a day.*

Belinda called an invitation to enter, dabbing at her tear-stained cheeks as she did so. Windsor stood there, rigid as always but with a softness to his face.

"I brought some tea, miss," he explained and moved into the room to set the tray on the low table.

Belinda stirred and murmured a thanks of sorts.

Windsor straightened—and then broke his code of many years, speaking personally to one he served.

"She had a great feeling for you, miss. You were to her as her own flesh and blood. She told me that often. And—and I know you loved her, too, miss. We all did."

He hesitated.

"But—but she wouldn't want you grieving like this, miss. So hopelessly. She—she went as she would have chosen to go. Silently—quickly. Without pain or fuss. In her own bed. You must allow her the honor of dignity, miss. Even in her dying."

Another pause. Windsor had Belinda's complete attention now.

"And one more thing, miss," he went on softly. "She was ready to meet her Lord. If it had happened before—even a month ago—she may not have been ready. We have you to thank for that, miss—and I thank you with all my heart."

Windsor bowed and was gone before Belinda could comment.

Somehow they all managed to muddle through one day after another. The house seemed to run without Belinda giving it much thought. She had little knowledge of what made such a big house run smoothly, so she was more than willing to let the staff continue on in their own way.

"What do I do now?" became her constant question. She supposed the staff as well was asking the question about her. They all would continue in their present positions for some period of time until the estate was settled. But she no longer had a position.

When she was able to reason clearly again, she sat down on a bench beside a bed of Thomas's roses to try to think through her situation.

Aunt Virgie is gone, she began. *There is no longer reason for me to stay here.*

She plucked a rose petal from the grass and held it to her lips. Then a new idea came to her, and she wondered why she hadn't thought of it immediately.

I'll go home, of course, she determined. *Back to where I belong.* The plan pleased her.

But then, *I don't really fit there anymore. When I was home for my visit, I felt like—like I didn't belong. I am too used to fine living—a big house, nice things.*

But even as the truth of it all came boldly to Belinda, she flinched. "I don't want to be like that," she declared out loud to herself. "I haven't any business being pampered and spoiled."

Her thoughts continued. *That's not of God. I came here to help an elderly lady who needed my nursing skills. I did that to the best of my ability. Now that she's gone, I'm no longer needed here. Surely—surely God won't allow me to just curl up in an easy chair and forget about the rest of the world.*

Belinda was sure God had something else—some other task for her to do.

I'm going back home, she said to herself determinedly. *The staff can continue running the house without me. I'm going home.*

Belinda had not yet worked out what she might do at home. That was the next question she tackled.

I'll do as Luke said, she decided. *I'll find a new spot for myself. I may not fit where I once was, but I need to find my roots again. I'll find a new place of service. It might take me awhile to sort it all out—but with God's help, I'll do it.*

With her resolve firmly in place, Belinda returned to the Manor. A wonderful peace had settled over her. At least now she knew what she would do next. She would go home—back to family and friends—and find some way to serve God in her own small town.

Belinda said nothing to the staff. She had much to do. There would be all the sorting and packing, and she had to make train reservations and write to Luke. *Perhaps—just perhaps,* she reasoned, *he will be able to use a rather "out-of-shape" nurse.* She felt that it would take her awhile to get back into formal nursing again—to be able to put in a full day's work. *But I can do it. I'm strong and healthy. There is no reason I can't soon be a help to the practice.*

She certainly wouldn't need all the fancy silks and satins to go back with her to her hometown. Folks would think she was putting on airs if she were to be dressed in so fancy a manner. Belinda wanted no such distance between her and the other town people. *I'll have to find out what can be done with these dresses,* she thought.

But the first task was the letter. Belinda sat down at the small writing desk and pulled her stationery forward. She had just dipped her pen for the first stroke when there was a knock on the door. Ella entered when Belinda called "Come in."

"Windsor asked me to fetch you, miss," Ella apologized. "It seems the magistrate wishes to see you in the library. Windsor is preparing tea."

Belinda frowned as she left the room and made her way to the library. She assumed that this man had something to do with the affairs of the late Mrs. Stafford-Smyth. *But what have*

I to do with that? Do they have some questions concerning the death? I was, after all, the nurse—though I was not present right at the time. Still, Belinda realized, if there were questions, it was logical to ask the attending medical person.

Nervously she smoothed her gown and made her way down the stairs. She found Mrs. Stafford-Smyth's attorney seated at the big oak desk in the library. He looked quite at home there. Belinda had seen him on more than one occasion.

He rose as Belinda entered the room and motioned her to a chair before him. Then he turned to acknowledge a second gentleman who sat in a chair by the fireplace. "Mr. Brown is our witness," he explained, which made no sense at all to Belinda.

Belinda settled herself in silence and waited for Mr. Dalgardy to begin.

He cleared his throat noisily and tapped his finger on the oak. Then he looked at Belinda over the rims of his glasses and cleared his throat again.

"We have the matter of the will," he said without emotion. "It is time for us to take some action."

Belinda nodded, wondering what it had to do with her. And then the man began to read in a droning, monotonous voice, legal jargon and long, strange words that meant absolutely nothing to Belinda.

Why is he doing this? Belinda wondered. *I don't understand a thing he is saying—and it really has nothing to do with me.*

There was a pause in the reading while Windsor brought in the tea service. Belinda poured and the reading went on.

Eventually a few items began to make sense to Belinda. There was a generous amount stated for both Franz and Pierre. The attorney assured Belinda that he would care for the matter, while she watched him with wide-eyed puzzlement. There were certain items left to each member of the household staff and a provision made for their future. That made sense. Belinda had been sure Mrs. Stafford-Smyth would not leave her staff in need.

And then the man read on. "And to Miss Belinda Davis, my loyal nurse and dear friend, I leave the remainder of my estate in its entirety—" The voice went on but Belinda heard no more.

She gasped and leaned forward in her chair, her hands turning cold and her face becoming pale.

"Why, whatever does she mean?" she managed to ask.

The attorney stopped reading to look at the girl.

"She never discussed it with you?" he asked simply.

"No," said Belinda, shaking her head emphatically in her innocence. "No."

"She means—just as it says—that to you she leaves everything that hasn't been previously disposed of."

"But—but—what is that? I don't understand—"

"I'm afraid it is much more than we can go into just now," answered the magistrate. "The house, the investments, the bank account. We will specify all of it in detail for you in due time."

"The house?" gasped Belinda. "This *house*?"

The man nodded. He was rather enjoying the effect he was having on the young girl. Clearly she was taken totally by surprise.

"This house." He had a difficult time to keep the composure befitting his position.

"Oh, my!" said Belinda, her hands to her lips as she leaned back helplessly in her chair. "Oh, my. There must be—there must be some mistake. Why, whatever in the world would I do with this house?"

She closed her eyes and pressed her hand to her forehead, hoping that the room would soon stop spinning.

Chapter 13

Decisions

"I—I think I need a few minutes alone," Belinda managed and the elder solicitor smiled in spite of himself.

"Of course," he answered in a fatherly tone. "Of course. I hadn't realized all this would be such a shock to you. We'll come back tomorrow—say two o'clock?"

Belinda managed a nod in agreement.

"Windsor will show you out," she said numbly, and fumbled for the doorknob.

Belinda fled to the coolness of the gardens, her head spinning, her brain dazed. She lowered herself onto a white wrought-iron bench beneath a lilac bush and tried to clear her fuzzy thinking.

This bush was covered with blossoms this spring, she murmured to herself. Such a strange thought under the circumstances. Belinda reached a hand to the greenery, fingering a leaf. *There's nothing here now—nothing. You wouldn't even know it had ever bloomed. Thomas has clipped all the seed pods.*

"How time changes," she whispered. "Seasons come and go—life begins and stops. A person has such a short time to make any impression on the world."

It could have been a morbid thought, but to Belinda it was one of action. It helped her to put things into proper perspective. It helped to clear her foggy brain.

"And now I have this—this to contend with," she said,

111

speaking aloud in the quiet garden. "I was going home. Had my mind all made up, and now—now I'm trapped." Belinda paused to stare mournfully at the lilac bush.

"She didn't intend for it to be a burden—she didn't mean to force me into a difficult circumstance. She thought she was doing me a favor—giving me an honor. But it isn't so. I don't want her house—her money. I never wanted it. I stayed because she was here and needed me—and now—now I am still not free to go."

Belinda lowered her head into her hands and began to weep. "Oh, dear," she cried. "Oh, dear. What do I do now? What do I do now?"

With heavy steps and a heavier heart, Belinda found her way to her room. She sat by the window with her Bible. A favorite psalm helped to quiet her heart and then she prayed. When she arose she washed her face, groomed her hair and went to the north parlor where she rang the bell and waited for Windsor. Her face was still pale, but her lips were firm in determination.

"Windsor, summon the staff, please," she ordered.

It was only a matter of minutes before they all stood before her. Belinda hardly knew where to begin.

"I suppose you know that an attorney paid us a visit today," she began. There was no reaction, and Belinda knew that the household had been well aware of the fact.

"Well, he brought some startling news," Belinda went on. "He read a portion of—of Madam's will."

Silence.

"In it she made provision for each of you. I'm sure that the matter will be presented to each of you at the proper time and circumstance. The will also said that—that she left the house and—and other things—to me."

No one in the room seemed the least surprised. There were a few murmurs of acceptance, even approval.

"Well, I have no idea—none whatever—of how to run a house such as this. But together we'll manage somehow. I just felt that—that each of you deserved to know how things stand. You all have your positions—as in the past. There will be no dismissals or rearranging of duties."

Belinda looked nervously around the circle. Heads nodded, she saw relief on some faces.

"Well . . . that's all I have to say—for the moment," she concluded. "You may . . . may . . ." Belinda floundered. How did one dismiss the staff?

"Thank you," she finally said. "That is all."

The staff understood they could now leave and moved toward the door. All but Windsor. He stood at stiff attention until the others had left and then approached Belinda. With a slight bow he addressed her. "Would you care for tea now—M'lady?"

Belinda had never been so addressed before. She understood immediately what Windsor intended. She was now the mistress of the manor. He and the staff would treat her accordingly. Her word was now rule.

The idea made her flustered. It was hard for her to find her tongue. "Why—why—yes, please. That would be fine," she managed to answer.

Belinda accepted the tea from the hand of the butler a few moments later. She didn't feel like sipping tea. She felt even less like tasting the tea biscuits that accompanied it, but she went through the motions.

Am I to sit each day, pretending to be something I'm not? she chafed. *I will go stark mad. No company. No duties. Nothing of worth accomplished. How will I ever bear such a life?*

Belinda set aside her teacup and slowly went back up to her room.

The two attorneys returned the next day as promised. After time with Belinda during which more details of the will were explained, the entire staff was called so that the portion of the will outlining their future provisions could be read to them. Belinda noticed some tears and heard such comments as, "She was so thoughtful," "Such a deah thing," and "My, how we will miss her."

Belinda had gone into a new kind of shock. On her young and inexperienced shoulders fell the task of running a large estate. An estate she had not asked for—one she did not wish.

Yet she knew she could not walk out on the new responsibility after having been entrusted with it in good faith. To do so would be an offense to the memory of the deceased. *But what am I to do?* Belinda asked herself over and over. *Grow old in this big house—all by myself?*

One morning Sarah came to her hesitantly. "M'lady," she said warily. "I was sent by Pottah to clean M'lady's—Madam's rooms—and I picked up her Bible and this fell out. It's addressed to you. I—I thought you should see it—M'lady."

Belinda reached for the envelope. It did bear her name.

She stood staring down at the handwriting of Mrs. Stafford-Smyth, fearful to open it, yet knowing she must. She reached for a letter opener from her desk and carefully slit the envelope, lifting from it a sheet of paper. Belinda's hands were trembling as she held the carefully penned note.

My dear Belinda:

I have no idea when you might be reading this, for at the moment of writing I feel just fine. However, I am reminded that at my age, one must always be prepared.

I have talked with my barrister again today, and I believe that we have all things in order. I realize that parts of my will might be a shock to you.

Had things been different, I would have left more of the responsibilities to my grandsons, but never mind that.

I am leaving most of what has been accumulated in my name to you, dear. This is not to be an "albatross," but a means for ministering. I know that you will, with your good sense, find a way to use it wisely. I leave all of the decisions to you. I trust you completely.

And, my dear, feel no grief or sorrow for me. I have gone to a much better place—thanks to your constant prompting that caused me to recognize the truth.

I have loved you as a daughter. I thank you for your love for me. You have filled the lonely days of an old woman with meaning—and a reason for living. I could never, never repay you.

All my love,
Virginia Stafford-Smyth.

Belinda's eyes were so tear-filled that she could hardly decipher the last few paragraphs. She grasped the letter, as a terrible loneliness for the writer besieged her.

She turned back to the penned lines again and reread the letter.

"This is not to be an 'albatross' but a means for ministering," she read aloud. "What did she mean?" Belinda wondered. "What was she trying to tell me?"

And then it came to her in a flash of insight. Mrs. Stafford-Smyth was not demanding that she stay in the house—had not even expected her to do so. She had left the house and funds to Belinda so she would put it to some good use. *Of course! It would be selfish—and foolish—to let this huge home and all the rooms sit idle and empty when so many people needed a roof over their heads. There is some way—there has to be some way—that it can be used to help people.*

A smile began to play around Belinda's lips and a new excitement burned in her heart.

"I need to have a good talk with an attorney," she said to herself. "I'm going to need lots of ideas and help to get this going properly."

Belinda felt she should share her ideas with the household staff. After all, their future was involved in her plans as well. She called them together again after the evening meal.

"Sarah found a letter this morning while cleaning Madam's rooms," she began. "It was addressed to me, but I think you all deserve to hear it," and Belinda proceeded to read the message. She skipped a paragraph or two, feeling that those sections were personal and need not be shared.

The staff listened attentively while Belinda read, but really seemed to feel that there was no new revelation there. Belinda was forced to explain—as she had known she would—her understanding of the line about the "albatross" and the "means for ministering."

"Mrs. Stafford-Smyth had no intention of my keeping this beautiful big house to waste on my own comfort," Belinda informed them. "She wanted me to use it to help others."

Questioning eyes turned toward her. She hurried on. "Now, I have no clear idea how to do that at present. I'm going to need the help of a law firm to discover just what can be done and what would be advised. I just wanted you all to know that I plan to find some way to share the Manor with others."

Expressions of both excitement and consternation filled the faces arrayed in front of Belinda.

"I want you to know, too," she continued, undaunted, "that I won't make any final decision until we have discussed it together. It is your home, too. I want you all to be in agreement with what is done here."

The ones who were anxious looked a bit relieved by the time Belinda dismissed them. She could imagine that there was a good deal of discussion once they reached the back rooms.

Belinda was weary—very weary. There had been so much happening in her life in the last few weeks. And now she had to begin a serious search of Boston for the proper attorney. She dreaded the ordeal, but she would start first thing in the morning.

Belinda had Windsor take her directly to the law firm that had represented Mrs. Stafford-Smyth. Windsor had phoned ahead for an appointment, and Mr. Dalgardy, who had visited the Manor with the will, greeted her in his office.

"And how may I serve you?" he asked graciously.

"It's concerning the will of Mrs. Virginia Stafford-Smyth," Belinda began.

"Yes-s. I assumed it was," the learned man nodded.

"Well, I—that is, you see the will—it doesn't say that I must keep the house. It just says that I have been *left* the house."

"I don't understand," said the man with a frown.

"Well," Belinda went on. "I also have a letter, you see—"

"Could I see the letter?"

"Well, I—I didn't bring it with me. It was a personal letter," stammered Belinda.

"Was it from the deceased?" asked the gentleman, "or some other party?"

"Oh, the deceased—for sure. I recognized her handwriting at once."

"I will need to see the letter, I'm afraid, if I am to verify that," the man replied distantly.

"Well, it doesn't change the will any. I mean—it just—it just explains some things—to me," hastily explained Belinda.

The man just continued to frown.

"Well, what I mean is—I don't think Mrs. Stafford-Smyth expected me to just—just live at the Manor—all alone and—and selfishly. I think she meant for me to use it in some way—to help others."

Mr. Dalgardy looked doubtful but he nodded for Belinda to go on.

"Well, I—I need to know what one could do with such a house. How one could put it to good use without—without destroying what—what it is now. And the staff—they still need to be able to carry on there as before, you see."

"You want it turned into a public museum?" asked the man.

"Oh, no. No, not at all. I don't think Aunt Virgie—Mrs. Stafford-Smyth—had that in mind at all."

"Then what did she have in mind?"

"Well, I don't know for sure. But it would mean helping people—I *am* sure of that. But I don't know what possibilities there are. That's why I need direction—advice. I need to know what the city would allow—what options one would have."

"I see," said the gentleman, shaking his head slowly.

Belinda was confused. His lips seemed to be saying one thing and his head quite another.

He rose from his chair and cleared his throat. "If you wish the house used to support charity," he began stiffly, "you can always sell it and donate the proceeds."

"But that wouldn't include the staff, you see," Belinda argued.

"They could be given an adequate pension," he maintained.

"Oh, but the house is their *home*—has been for ever so many years. I don't think—"

"I'm sorry," the attorney interrupted, standing, "that's the only way I could help you."

Belinda realized she was being dismissed.

She rose shakily to her feet. "I . . . I see," she murmured, as she straightened her skirt and lifted her parasol. She was almost out the door before the man called after her, "If you decide you'd like to sell, I might be able to find a buyer."

Belinda lifted her chin and sailed out the door. *Over my dead body,* she fumed inwardly. *I'll never sell Marshall Manor right out from under the entire staff.*

Chapter 14

The Task

Keen disappointment colored Belinda's voice as she relayed to Windsor the news of her visit with the attorney. She didn't know where to turn next. But Windsor didn't give up as easily.

"Did you ask Mr. Dalgardy if there was a law firm he might recommend?" he asked Belinda.

She shook her head. "I didn't even think of it," she admitted. "I guess I was just too—too upset when he mentioned selling Marshall Manor. Why, I shouldn't be surprised but that he had his eye on it himself," she snapped indignantly.

Windsor made no reply. He never would have said so, but he wouldn't be one bit surprised either. Marshall Manor was noted as one of the leading properties in the city.

"Well, I suppose we must just go from law office to law office," the butler said matter-of-factly. "I know of no shortcuts."

Belinda sighed.

The day was already hot. She was glad she had brought her parasol.

"Will we need appointments?" she asked, apprehensive. "If we have to make an appointment with each law firm, we could be at it for months."

"Usually," Windsor replied, "but they might give some information. At least we could get the name of whom to call from the secretary."

Belinda nodded. "How shall I do it?" she asked.

119

"Well, M'lady, if you like, I will take those two offices across the street. You try the one at hand. I will ask for information on your behalf, and you could ask if this one is interested in governing your affairs."

Belinda nodded. It sounded simple enough. She gathered up her skirts for the long climb up the stairs to her assigned firm. She could see their sign: Browne, Browne and Thorsby, Barristers and Solicitors.

By the time she reached the office door, she was breathless and perspiring. She paused long enough to wipe her brow, regain her composure, and then tapped on the door.

"Come in," a male voice invited.

Belinda trembled slightly as she approached the large, littered desk. She tried to remember how Windsor had suggested she express her case, but she couldn't.

"I'm Belinda—Miss Davis," she said. "I am looking for a barrister—an attorney who will help me—with the—the administration of an estate."

"Do you have an appointment?" the man asked curtly, peering sternly over his glasses.

"No—I—"

"We do not accept off-the-street business," the man informed her firmly.

"But I—I—" began Belinda, but stopped at his frank stare. *Off-the-street!* she murmured to herself. It sounded so coarse— so vulgar. For one moment she returned the man's bold look, and then she colored, spun on her heel, and left the office.

Down, down the long stairway she descended, her flush heightening with each step.

What a crude way of responding, she muttered to herself. *I do hope Windsor is treated with more respect.*

But Windsor had fared no better. It was a discouraging report he brought to Belinda.

"I think we'd best go home, M'lady," he advised. "We will need to spend some time sorting this through if we are to gain admittance."

Belinda agreed. She was hot and tired. And she was in no mood to be "put down" any further today.

She did not even notice the beauty of the fall day as the carriage wound its way through the city streets and back to the grand home in the well-to-do section of town.

They spent a great deal of time making calls, following up one possibility after another, making trips to the inner city and rapping on doors and ringing doorbells. But to Belinda's thinking, they were no nearer to solving their dilemma than when they began. She was beginning to feel that they might as well give up when the minister of the local church made an afternoon call.

"I understand that Marshall Manor has been left in your capable hands," he commented with a charming smile.

And you wish to be sure that you and your church stand in favorable light, Belinda thought but did not say. She chided herself for even thinking such thoughts. After all, he was a man of the cloth, and it was due to his sermon that Mrs. Stafford-Smyth had made peace with her God before her death. He was, Belinda admitted, preaching from the Holy Scripture, even if his application was ineffectual, to her way of thinking.

She nodded silently, waiting for the man to go on.

"We at the church just want you to know that, as Mrs. Stafford-Smyth before you, we value you as a member of our congregation. And if there is ever any way we can be of service—"

"As a matter of fact," Belinda cut in on sudden impulse, "there might be a way. I am in need of an attorney. As you can imagine, this—this house and estate—well, they involve a great many decisions. And—well, I'm not really used to making such judgments on my own. I feel the need for a good attorney to help me in such matters. Would you know of anyone who might be interested in helping me?"

Belinda did not know that any law firm in the city would have been more than eager to help had they known just who she was and the size of her estate. Nor did she know how to approach such firms.

"I . . . I think that I might be able to help you," he said with only slight hesitation. "I'll do some inquiring and see what I can discover."

Belinda thanked him sincerely, and the parson went on his way.

And so it was that three days later there was another caller at Marshall Manor.

Windsor opened the door and waited while the man admired the wonderful face of the building, the lovely lawns and the flower beds. Windsor cleared his throat and the man produced a card. "The Rev. Arthur Goodbody informed me that the lady of the house is seeking legal advice," he told Windsor, and Windsor nodded, stepped aside and ushered the man in.

"I shall call M'lady," he said curtly. "You may wait in the library."

The attorney smiled, followed the butler, and accepted a seat as indicated.

Belinda could hardly believe the good news Windsor brought to her as he handed her the attorney's card.

"The parson has sent him, M'lady," he explained.

"Oh, bless his soul!" exclaimed Belinda. "I had most given up," and she hastened to the library to meet the gentleman.

When Belinda entered the room, her face flushed, skirts swishing, the attorney was staring at the thousands of books displayed on the shelves, his expression appropriately impressed. The man rose to his feet as manners dictated, but then a frown replaced the admiration on his face.

"I'm Belinda—Miss Davis," Belinda said with a smile. "And you are"— she referred to the card in her hand—"Keats, Cross and Newman," she read out loud and then smiled again. "Which one?" she asked frankly.

"The—the Keats one," the man answered haltingly. "Anthony Keats."

"I'm so pleased you have consented to offer your services," Belinda began and then realized they were still standing. "Please be seated," she said, then walked behind the big oak desk and sat down in the chair.

The man looked bewildered, but he sat down.

"I guess I should explain—briefly," Belinda went on. "I want to put this property to good use. But I don't know how to go about it properly. And I don't know my options—my limits. I need legal aid—advice—to help with some major decisions."

"I see," returned the gentleman, but he didn't sound as if he saw at all.

"It's a big house—very big. I haven't even counted the bedrooms," Belinda continued, embarrassed. "Of course some of them are needed by the staff. The staff is to stay on," she hurriedly explained. "This—this is their home, too."

The man nodded.

"Of course, I won't be here. I plan to go home just as soon—just as soon as I can get this all settled."

"Could I speak with the homeowner?" the man asked cautiously.

Belinda reddened. "But I am the owner," she maintained. "That's why I have called you here."

"Ma'am," the attorney said, stopping Belinda cold, "this is a legal matter. I will need some legal papers."

"Like—?"

"A deed."

"Oh, you mean to the house? Yes, I have it now. It was just delivered last week. It is right here," and Belinda crossed to a safe in the wall. When she had opened it with a click, Belinda removed some documents and handed them to the lawyer. He studied each carefully, his eyes darting from the papers to Belinda and back again.

"How did you obtain the house?" he finally asked her.

"Aunt Virgie—Mrs. Stafford-Smyth—left it to me in her will."

"Your—your aunt?"

"Well, not my aunt—not legally. I just called her Aunt Virgie. I worked for her. I was her nurse—and her friend," Belinda explained.

The frown on the lawyer's face deepened. "And now you wish to dispose of the house?" he asked.

"Yes," said Belinda.

"Because you can't afford to maintain it?" questioned the man.

It was Belinda's turn to frown.

"Do you need the money?" the lawyer asked outright.

"Oh, no," Belinda hastened to inform him. "She left a good deal of money along with the house."

The attorney took a deep breath. "You—you just wish to be rid of it? To sell?"

"Oh, I don't want to sell," Belinda told him. "My, no. I would never sell Marshall Manor. I just want to—to put it to good use. Aunt Virgie said I could—in her letter."

The attorney looked perplexed. Belinda smiled. "Perhaps we should start over," she offered. "We both seem confused."

The man laughed then. "Perhaps we should."

"Here," said Belinda, handing him a package. "Here is the will—and the letter. Read it while I ring for some tea. I feel in need of some. Perhaps you would join me."

Belinda gave Mr. Keats plenty of time to study the legal document and the note. When he laid it aside and removed his spectacles, Belinda began again. "Do you understand now?"

"Understand? No. But things are certainly in order. You have the will, the deed. You are free to do whatever you wish with the property."

That much was good news to Belinda.

Windsor brought the tea tray and Belinda poured and served the beverage to the gentleman.

"Now, what I need to know is—what ways are there for me to put this house to good use?"

"You mean—like a public museum, with an entrance fee?"

Belinda shook her head impatiently. *Why does everyone think that I want to use it for income?* she muttered inwardly. *I have no intention of desecrating Aunt Virgie's home for money.* To the gentleman before her she said, "I want to use the home for good. As a means of ministry—just like Aunt Virgie said in the letter."

"In—in what manner, ma'am—er, miss?"

"I don't know," responded Belinda. "That's why I need your advice."

"I see," said the gentleman, sounding a bit impatient.

There was a moment of silence.

"It would help me tremendously, miss, if I had some—some idea as to what you have in mind," Mr. Keats stated at last.

"Well—well, I don't know exactly," responded Belinda. "But—it seems to me that with so many homeless on the streets and all of these lovely rooms here that—well, that there should be some way to get the two together."

The man looked shocked. "You mean—like—like an overnight hostel?" he queried.

"No, no. Something more permanent than that. So much coming and going would likely ruin the house—and run the staff to death. We can't do anything like that."

The man seemed relieved.

"But there must be some way to put this lovely place to good use," determined Belinda. The man rose to his feet and returned the package of legal documents to her. "I'll look into it," he promised.

"Oh, thank you," replied Belinda sincerely. "I was about to give up in despair—and I do so much want to get this finalized and return home."

Mr. Keats cast a glance all around him. "The house is beautiful. Frankly, I can't imagine your ever wanting to leave it. But I'll call as soon as I have some ideas," he assured her, and then Windsor was there to show the man out.

Chapter 15

Dinner

"How nice," murmured Belinda as her eyes quickly scanned the formal invitation in her hand. "It's from Mrs. Prescott," she said, lifting her head to speak to Windsor. "She has asked me to dinner next Thursday."

Windsor gave a slight nod. "You will wish the carriage, M'lady?"

Belinda thought for a moment. "Oh, dear," she said. "I don't even know where Mrs. Prescott lives."

"Mrs. Prescott was never much for entertaining, miss. She came here often, but she was always much too busy—" Windsor caught himself and began to gather up the tea things. "I know the way, M'lady," he said instead. "I have driven Madam a number of times in the past."

The mention of Mrs. Stafford-Smyth brought a shadow to Belinda's face. An evening spent with Celia Prescott might be very painful. It was bound to bring back many memories of their times together in the past. Belinda wondered if she was quite ready for such an occasion. She stirred restlessly, then rose from her chair and walked to the unlit fireplace. She stood rubbing agitated hands, her eyes staring into the ashes, though actually seeing little. Windsor turned to look at her.

"Maybe I . . . maybe I should just decline the . . . the invitation," she said hesitantly.

"Madam would not wish that, miss," Windsor replied softly, evenly.

Belinda looked up quickly, surprised that he had voiced his opinion so frankly.

"No-o," she conceded. "No—I don't suppose she would. But it's—it's going to be so difficult—"

Windsor nodded.

"Do you miss her—terribly much?" Belinda suddenly burst out.

For a moment there was only silence; then Windsor nodded his head. "Terribly!" he answered, then spun around and was gone with the tea things.

Belinda stood looking down into the empty fireplace. *Ashes,* she thought. *Only ashes where once there was a warm and living flame. It's rather symbolic. Oh, I miss her.*

She brushed tears from her eyes and left the fireplace to cross to the window. In the gardens Thomas was working over a flower bed, McIntyre curled up on the lawn beside him, head on paws. The elderly man and his dog seemed such a natural part of the landscape.

Belinda smiled softly. It was a beautiful day and Windsor was right, she admitted. Mrs. Stafford-Smyth would not want her to sit at home. She, Belinda, had to get on with life.

She went to the corner desk and settled down to write her acceptance of the dinner invitation. Then she tucked the note into an envelope, left it on the hall table for Windsor to deliver, and went out to the gardens to see Thomas.

Belinda prepared carefully for the dinner engagement. She felt a great deal of excitement and no small measure of curiosity. Why was the elderly woman inviting her to dinner? It was true that while Mrs. Stafford-Smyth was living, she regarded Celia Prescott as one of her dearest friends. It was also true that during the time Belinda had lived at Marshall Manor, they had not been invited to the Prescott home. Belinda had heard the ladies refer to times in the past when they had shared dinner or tea at the Prescotts', but it had seemed that Mrs. Prescott was no longer disposed to formal entertaining. "It just takes so much out of one," Belinda had once heard Mrs. Prescott tell Mrs. Stafford-Smyth.

So why now? Belinda asked herself again. *And why me?* Perhaps Mrs. Prescott realized how deeply Belinda was missing their dear mutual friend. Or perhaps Mrs. Prescott herself was feeling keenly the loss. *At any rate, an evening out will be good,* Belinda decided. She attended church services on Sunday and went on an occasional shopping trip, but that was the extent of her outings. Even a beautiful house could become a bit wearisome.

Belinda looked at her reflection in the mirror. The dark blue silk was becoming. As Belinda smoothed the rich material over her hip line, she remembered a comment Mrs. Stafford-Smyth had once made. "I don't want anyone ever going into mourning black for me," she had said. "When people think of me, I want them to think colah. Brightness, not morbid black. You weah colah—blues, greens, crimsons—you heah me, deah?"

Belinda had laughed at the time. Mrs. Stafford-Smyth had not looked like a lady about to bid farewell to life. But then she had gone—so suddenly. As Belinda studied her mirrored reflection and the blue silk, she thought again of her former employer's lighthearted words.

"I know you would approve, Aunt Virgie," Belinda whispered softly. "But will others understand?"

Belinda sighed. Celia Prescott might not understand.

Belinda rang for Ella. *Tonight I will have my hair styled,* she decided.

Windsor was waiting when Belinda went down. The evening was warm and the air heavy with the scent of flowers when she climbed aboard the carriage. She was tempted to tell Windsor to just drive—anywhere. It was good to be out. It was good to drink in the loveliness of the neighborhood gardens. It was good to just escape for a few moments and forget the heaviness of her heart. She realized that she was actually looking forward to conversation around the dinner table—even if the other guests would be three or four times her age. One of the things she dreaded most about each day was eating dinner all alone.

Soon the carriage was pulling up before a wide entrance.

Belinda stared at the ornate columns, the blue-gray shutters, the windows long and lean, the lines graceful. It was a pretty house—though not nearly as magnificent as Marshall Manor.

Windsor assisted Belinda from the carriage. "I shall pass the time with Mallone," he informed her. "Have Chiles ring when you are ready."

Belinda gave Windsor a brief nod and was soon being admitted by Chiles himself. Mrs. Prescott appeared in the hallway, bubbling and light as always.

"My deah girl," she enthused, "how have you been? I've been thinking of you—constantly."

Belinda murmured her thanks and allowed herself to be drawn into the parlor.

"You look just lovely, my deah," Mrs. Prescott went on. "Just lovely. And so right. I know how Virgie felt about black. She called it a 'disgusting colah.'" Mrs. Prescott laughed heartily at the recollection.

"But come, my deah," she said. "I want you to meet someone."

Mrs. Prescott drew her toward the chairs before the fireplace, and a young man rose to his feet. Belinda had not noticed him when she entered the room. And he certainly had not made his presence known. He looked embarrassed about greeting her now. He extended a hand, quickly pulled it back and tucked it awkwardly behind his back, then slowly began to extend it again.

"Belinda, my nephew, Morton Jamison," Mrs. Prescott beamed. "Morton, this is the delightful young lady I was telling you about."

Morton flushed and fully extended his nervous hand. Belinda took it momentarily and gave a customary shake. "How do you do?" she greeted him with a smile. He muttered in return and self-consciously wiped his hand down the length of his dinner jacket.

"Morton is studying at Yale," went on Mrs. Prescott, and Morton flushed a deeper red.

"I see," commented Belinda. "How nice." She attempted an encouraging smile. The young man was really uncomfortably shy. Belinda felt sorry for him and wished to put him at ease.

"Please, please be seated," she smiled and moved to take a chair herself. With a look of great relief the young man sat down.

"What are you studying?" Belinda inquired.

"I—I haven't really decided," the young man stammered. "Maybe—maybe business—maybe law. I—"

"Morton has his daddy's business to run—someday," cut in Mrs. Prescott. "Right now he's preparing himself with a broad background."

Belinda nodded. "How wise," she agreed and gave the man another smile.

Belinda found her eyes scanning the room. It would appear that she was early. Other guests had not as yet arrived. Belinda had already decided that she didn't plan to develop the habit of lateness, as Celia Prescott seemingly had done. She turned back to her hostess, who was speaking again.

"I thought it would be nice for you young folks to get to know one anothah, being the same age—and you alone in that big house and all," she was saying. "You must get awfully lonely."

"That's very kind," Belinda said softly. "I do get lonely at times."

"Well, you just count on us—me and Morton, anytime, deah," fluttered Mrs. Prescott, and Morton shuffled uneasily in his chair.

Chiles entered the room, cleared his throat and announced "Dinnah is served, madam" in a tight, squeaky voice.

Mrs. Prescott nodded and bounced up. "Well, well, now. Let's go right in."

Young Morton seemed totally confused. He acted as if he didn't know if he was to escort his Aunt Celia or the young lady dinner guest. Mrs. Prescott took charge. "I'll lead the way, Morton, and you bring Miss Belinda," she directed. Morton moved to hesitantly offer Belinda his arm, his neck red with embarrassment.

Belinda ached for the young man. He was so obviously ill-at-ease that she could only sympathize with him. She gave him a smile and fell into step beside him.

His build was slight, making him seem shorter than he actually was, Belinda noticed. His chin was sharp, his nose a bit too long, his mouth too large, his eyes squinty and hidden behind rimmed glasses, his hair stiff and awkward looking. These features taken alone would not have been a problem, but combined as they were on the young man, they did not make an attractive whole.

Perhaps he is so unsure of himself because he is so plain, reasoned Belinda, determined that she would do her best to set the young man at ease.

"I thought it would be nice to have just a cozy little chitchat," Mrs. Prescott explained as she took her place at the table and motioned Belinda to her right, the young man to her left.

Sitting directly across from the young man proved to be more unsettling than if she had sat next to him, Belinda decided. His nervousness was even more apparent when he was forced to meet her eyes. As a result, Belinda, too, became self-conscious and found it difficult to converse.

Fortunately for the dinner party, Celia Prescott never seemed to run out of things to say. She chatted endlessly throughout the meal, the other two giving an occasional nod or acknowledgment. But as the evening progressed, it became more and more apparent that she had "set up" the dinner as an opportunity for the two young people to "become acquainted." Belinda began to feel more and more uncomfortable.

"A young woman like you, attractive and poised, ought to be married," said the frank Mrs. Prescott. "And it does seem such a pity that you should bear the whole burden of caring for such a big house and estate all on you-ah own. I told Morton heah that one who has had some training in business affaihs should be handling all of that fuss. My word! I nevah would have wanted to care foah the business end of things like my Wilbur was expected to do. So many things to considah. Now— well, I just live heah. The trust takes care of all the details. I . . ." and she rambled on and on.

Belinda was beginning to get the picture. "Oh, I really don't mind the business details at all," she put in. "I do have a reliable attorney. It makes it much easier. And I also have an excellent staff. They can care for the house and grounds quite well on their own."

Mrs. Prescott looked a trifle disconcerted. "But still," she hastened on, "a young woman like you needs a—a husband—family. Surely you don't want to live all you-ah life alone. Why—"

Belinda smiled. "Perhaps living alone is preferred to living with—with an unsuitable mate," she said evenly. Morton shuffled uncomfortably. It was clear he felt he was being discussed. *Oh dear,* thought Belinda, annoyed with herself. *I hadn't meant—I only meant—*

Belinda felt sorry for the young man and tried to change the direction of the conversation. "Do you plan to travel this winter, Mrs. Prescott?" she asked.

It took the older woman a few moments to change the direction of her thoughts. At last she was able to respond. "No—no, I think not—though I really haven't given it much thought at all. I—I well, it's early yet. I often don't make my plans until much latah."

"Have you seen the new play at the theater?" asked Belinda, determined not to let the conversation return to its former topic.

"Yes—yes, I have. Twice, in fact," admitted the woman.

"Then it must be a good one," Belinda enthused, glad for something new to discuss.

"Well, not particularly," said Mrs. Prescott. "I often go two or three times—just for the outing. In fact, the play itself was rather mundane, but the company is always good. I enjoy the time out in the evening. It's always nice to be with othah people."

Belinda nodded and was about to make further comment when Mrs. Prescott went on. "And that's why I worry about you, deah. You nevah get out. Morton would be glad to escort you to the play, wouldn't you, Morton?" But without waiting for a reply she hurried on. "And there are any numbah of interesting museums and concerts and such that Morton would be happy to—"

"Oh, I have seen most of the museums," Belinda informed them easily. "When Pierre was home, Aunt Virgie arranged for us to go."

Mrs. Prescott's face clouded with the recollection. Belinda remembered that the woman had confronted her friend Virgie about letting her young grandson escort "common help" about Boston. Now she seemed to be trying to set up her nephew with that same young lady. Mrs. Prescott flushed slightly. "I'm sure that there are new displays since that time, my deah," she went on with an indulgent smile. "And one can nevah get too much music."

Belinda had to agree with that. She loved the concerts and did miss them.

"Well, for the moment, I am dreadfully busy," she replied with a smile. "I don't have time for concerts, or museums, or any such thing. I am totally taken with trying to make all the arrangements for the Marshall Manor—"

"That's just what I've been saying, deah," the older woman said with a hint of impatience. "Theah is absolutely no need for you to bothah you-ah pretty head with such things. A capable husband could care for all that. Why—"

But this time it was Morton who cut in. "Aunt Celia, I believe that Miss Davis is quite capable of making up her mind if—and when—she wishes to marry," he said with more spunk than Belinda would have given him credit for. "And I won't be available as escort because I am going back to Yale the first of the week."

"You said—you said you hadn't made up your mind," accused Mrs. Prescott.

"Well, I have now," the gentleman replied with determination. "And now I believe we are ready for our dessert. Would you like me to ring for Chiles?"

With a disgusted look Mrs. Prescott reached for the bell, and Belinda gave the young man a hint of a smile and a nod. Her respect for him had just risen tremendously, but a healthy measure of respect was all she felt.

Chapter 16

Arrangements

Belinda received a message from her attorney, Anthony
Keats. It said simply that he had investigated the possibilities
for the use of Marshall Manor and had some proposals to discuss. He would be happy to drop by the house if she'd like to
set a time. Belinda gave Windsor a few appointment times and
had him call the law office to arrange one. She found herself
getting more and more nervous as the appointed time drew
near.

Windsor opened the door to the man and ushered him into
the library where Belinda soon joined him. He looked pleased
with himself, and Belinda felt her pulse quicken as she asked
him to be seated and then took the chair directly across.

"I have done a good deal of looking into the matter," he
began.

Belinda listened with anticipation.

"The first possibility that came to mind was an orphanage,"
he began. Belinda wondered why she hadn't thought of it, but
even as she considered it she thought of the large staff an orphanage would take.

"Of course, an orphanage doesn't seem to fit too well with
such a decorous house," the man went on. "One would need to
completely strip the rooms and furnish them far more simply
and sell or dispose of all the—the ornate bric-a-brac. You

couldn't have children and all of the beautiful things trying to co-exist here."

Belinda followed his logic. It was unreasonable to expect children to live in such a setting. It was also very difficult to consider selling off all the things that Mrs. Stafford-Smyth had collected and viewed as a part of her home. Belinda shook her head sadly. It didn't seem like a good idea, after all.

"Now, another good possibility," the man went on, "would be a conservatory of sorts."

"A conservatory?"

"Music—the arts," the man said. "She did enjoy the arts, didn't she?"

"Oh, yes. Of course," responded Belinda. "But how—?"

"You could set this up for exceptional students. You have the music room for lessons, the library and three or four other rooms to convert to practice rooms. The bedrooms as boarding facilities. It would work very nicely for music."

Belinda sat very still. It was all such a new thought to her.

"Or any of the arts," he continued convincingly. "If you wished to set it up for painting, you could convert the front parlor to a—"

But Belinda stopped him with a shake of her head. She really didn't want to "convert" the house to anything. She was much more interested in using it the way it was.

"Well, you could set it up as a library. This part of town could use a good library. The front parlor would then be a reading room. The dining room and north parlor additional shelf space—" But Belinda was shaking her head again.

"You have already ruled out a museum," said the man, ill-concealed irritation in his voice.

Belinda nodded. To think of the house as an attraction for the curious just didn't seem right to her.

"I really would like it—*lived* in. In its present state," said Belinda.

The man sighed deeply. "Miss Davis, to do that, you may have to sell it," he reminded her. "Who would want—or *need*—a house this size? This—this elaborate?"

"It's not a good place for children," Belinda admitted. "They couldn't run and play freely. Staffing it would be a problem. I don't suppose it would work at all for children." She was talking more to herself than to the gentleman who sat before her.

But the man answered anyway. "Exactly! And the children are the only ones who would need such a place. Other folks have homes of their own."

Belinda nodded sadly. It seemed that her plan wasn't going to be workable, after all.

"You're right," she agreed with a sigh. "It's just the young— and the old—who often need a place to stay."

And then Belinda sat up straight in her chair. "That's it," she cried in excitement. "That's it!"

"I beg your pardon," said the man.

"The *elderly*. We can make it into a home for needy older folks. It will be perfect! They can enjoy all the pretty things. We won't need as many staff members as an orphanage would. They can live in dignity—with the company of others. They can walk in the gardens, sit in the sunshine. They will have the library, the music room. It's perfect."

The man watched her face. Belinda was really enthusiastic over her plan. At last he nodded slowly. "It might work," he decided. "If handled cautiously, carefully."

"Oh, yes," enthused Belinda.

"How many would you consider?" he asked.

"Six? Eight? No more than a dozen," answered Belinda.

"And how would you find the—the occupants?" he continued.

"I don't know, but churches—the city—someone must know of older folks with no homes of their own."

"They would need to be able to climb stairs," the man reminded Belinda.

"Maybe some sort of lift could be built," she suggested.

"It would mar the structure," he cautioned.

"We wouldn't need to put it in the front hall," Belinda countered. "There's plenty of room to put some arrangement off the north parlor or the library. We'll have someone take a look."

The lawyer nodded his head somewhat dubiously.

"What about help?" he asked. "Will your present household staff agree to such a plan?"

Belinda sobered. "I told them that I plan to do something with the house," she said slowly. "I will need to talk with them about this idea. I wouldn't want to do something against their wishes. This is their home, too."

The man nodded. "Do you want me to discuss it with them?" he asked.

"No. No, I will talk with them about the plan. I'd prefer it that way."

"Then I guess we have nothing more to consider until I hear further from you," the attorney said, tucking his sheaf of proposal papers back in his leather case and standing to his feet.

"I will be in touch," Belinda assured him. "And thank you. Thank you so much."

He didn't seem quite as excited as Belinda was.

Windsor was waiting beyond the library doors to show the gentleman out. As soon as the entrance door had closed, Belinda turned to the butler.

"We need a staff meeting—in the north parlor," she announced excitedly. "See if everyone can be gathered in fifteen minutes—and have Potter prepare tea—for all of us. Thomas, too, if he'll join us. No. No—not the parlor," Belinda changed her mind. The parlor was much too formal. "We'll meet on the back veranda." She would meet with her staff in a place where they felt more at ease.

Then Belinda hurried up the stairs to change into a simple gown. She wanted to talk as an equal with all the household. They had an important matter to discuss. One that would affect all their futures.

The staff had assembled on the veranda by the time Belinda returned. Some looked a bit uncomfortable and anxious as she made her appearance, but Belinda quickly attempted to make them feel at ease.

"Potter, would you pour, please?" she asked and settled herself on the top step, where she could look up rather than down on her staff.

"Ella, would you pass the cakes, please? And then we can get on with our discussion as soon as everyone finds a comfortable spot."

Thomas accepted his tea and joined Belinda on the step. McIntyre flopped down on the grass at his feet.

Windsor pushed a chair forward for Potter and another for Cook, then rather reluctantly took one himself. Ella and Sarah stood leaning against the veranda rail.

"I told you all that I hoped to keep Marshall Manor the same—but be able to put it to another use," began Belinda. "Well, the attorney whom I asked to look into the matter was here this morning." Belinda would not have needed to mention that bit of information. The whole household was well aware of the fact.

"Well, he had a number of suggestions. He proposed that we use it as a—a music or arts conservatory, or a library—or such. But for all those things the house would have to be altered— remodeled. Well, I don't favor changing it."

There were approving nods from some of the employees.

"We talked about an orphanage—" Belinda noticed nervous glances. "But that, too, would involve a great deal of alteration."

Belinda thought she heard sighs of relief.

"To me, the most logical thing would be to allow this to be a beautiful, natural home for the elderly," went on Belinda. "We could house a limited number of those who need homes. The house basically can be left as it is. All of the pretty things can be enjoyed. The occupants can stroll the garden paths, bask in the sun on the benches, or sit in the parlors and do handwork. Those who play can enjoy the piano. Or they can read in the library. And, the best part, there really wouldn't be that much we would need to change."

Belinda watched the faces in the circle around her. Their expressions had gone from concern, to doubt, to acceptance in a few short minutes.

Windsor spoke first. "Would the present staff be expected to proceed as formerly, M'lady?"

"All who wish to," responded Belinda. "Of course, we will

need more staff. There will be more people to feed—and care for."

A few more faces relaxed.

"T'won't nobody dig in my flower beds," mumbled Thomas.

Belinda laughed. "We'll keep all hands out of your flowers, Thomas, I promise you," she informed him. A few others chuckled along with her.

"But we would need more help in the kitchen and the laundry. And for the cleaning. I guess we should all sit down and take a good look at what will need doing and decide whose duty it will be. Then we will need to find additional staff. But—first I need to know your reaction to the plan."

Belinda let her eyes travel from face to face, but no one volunteered an opinion.

"Windsor, what do you think of the idea?" Belinda finally asked.

Windsor didn't hesitate. "Things will nevah be like they were in the past," he said evenly, "and there is no way to change that. I'm sure that after all consideration, the plan you have chosen is the best possible one, M'lady."

"And you'll stay on in your present capacity?"

Windsor nodded. "Yes, M'lady," he agreed.

"Good!" Belinda exclaimed, her relief evident. "Potter?"

"I couldn't leave the old house aftah so many years," the woman acknowledged, close to tears. "I'll stay."

"Thank you," said Belinda. "Cook?"

The woman just nodded, her feelings too close to the surface to speak.

"Sarah?"

"I've been meanin' to talk to you, miss," replied Sarah, blushing deeply. "I—I'm planning to be married—soon. I won't be staying on in any case." She lowered her face and moved one foot nervously across the veranda boards.

"Why, Sarah," exclaimed Belinda, rising quickly to her feet, "how wonderful! I am so happy for you." And she went to give the girl a hug. The whole group seemed to pick up the excitement, and a murmur ran through the staff.

It was a few moments until Belinda continued. "And you,

Ella? You aren't getting married, too, are you?" she teased.

Ella blushed. "Not as I've been informed, miss," she answered good-naturedly. "I'll be glad to stay."

"And, Thomas—you and McIntyre will remain caring for the grounds?" Belinda said with a straight face but a twinkle in her eye.

The old gardener grinned but McIntyre only stirred slightly and rearranged his head on his paws.

Belinda looked back at her staff. "I am so thankful—so relieved," she informed them sincerely. "You have all been invaluable to Mrs. Stafford-Smyth—and to me. I don't know how the house would ever manage without you." She paused, then said, "Now we will need to do some careful planning. Potter, I will want to talk to you at length about the staff requirements. And, Cook, I will need your help with the kitchen requirements. We have so much to do, but at least now we know how we should proceed. Thank you. Thank you all so much."

After giving Sarah one more hug, Belinda dismissed the staff.

The next weeks were busy ones at Marshall Manor. There were many decisions to be made, so many needs to be taken care of.

A contractor came to assess the possibility of a lift. He laid out a workable plan for the back hall at the end of the big library. The arrangement would work well both upstairs and down and not disturb the appearance of the house. He began the installation immediately. Belinda decided she would be very glad when the construction was over and the mess cleaned up. She could tell that Potter would be even more relieved. The housekeeper was nearly frantic during the building of the lift, trying to keep the dust out of "her" house.

After several discussions, it was decided that the house could accommodate ten residents without destroying its charm and character. Belinda hoped it wouldn't be too difficult to find the ten.

Legal papers had to be drawn up to cover all possible eventualities. Belinda had never seen so many forms and documents. She dreamed of smothering in stacks of papers, struggling to get a breath of air. The whole procedure turned out to be an exhausting as well as an exhilarating one. Belinda prayed for the day when it all would be taken care of and she would be free to return to her own home.

Chapter 17

The Unexpected

Belinda dressed carefully in her gray suit and pinned her hat securely on top of upswept hair. She frowned into her mirror, hoping she looked mature and responsible. She dreaded another trip to the law office. Her days seemed to be filled with legal documents and decisions. She was getting tired of it all.

Will it never end? she wondered for the hundredth time. She really wished Mrs. Stafford-Smyth had left the responsibility of her estate to the rightful heirs, her grandsons. Then Belinda checked herself. *Aunt Virgie was always so kind to me. Surely I can do this small kindness in return.* Belinda turned from her mirror and went down to see if Windsor had brought the carriage.

Belinda reminded herself as she looked about at the lovely autumn colors that this would be her last fall season in Boston. If things proceeded as she hoped, she would be out of Boston before another winter set in.

Belinda sighed deeply. She was so looking forward to getting home. She knew there would be many adjustments. She had left home Belinda Davis, young girl. She was going home as Belinda Davis, mature woman. She had done some foreign traveling, she had enjoyed cultural experiences in music and theater, her manners had been refined to eastern standards—and she had grown up. It would be very different for her in her hometown. She would need to find herself a new spot in the community and in the church life. *But I will do it,* she told herself. She would do it because she didn't want to lose all the worthwhile things her small-town roots had given her. Family. Deep friendships. Faith. Love. Acceptance. A regard for fellowmen not based on position or possessions. Belinda longed to return to simple absolutes.

When they reached the law office, Windsor helped her down and promised that he would return on the hour. Belinda shook the wrinkles from her long skirts, lifted a hand to be sure her hat was properly in place and began the climb to the law office on the second floor.

"Good afternoon, Miss Davis," a male receptionist addressed her. She had been in touch with this office so often she was now known by name. She nodded and offered a greeting.

"Mr. Keats will be with you shortly," he said. Belinda moved to a chair in the waiting area and sat down.

Are we really getting any nearer to finishing all these arrangements? she asked herself as she pulled off her gloves. *Each time I think the end should be in sight, some new decisions and more papers are needed. Oh, I hope this will all be over soon.*

"Miss Davis," Mr. Keats summoned her into his office. He was beaming, and Belinda hoped it meant much had been accomplished.

"Well, I believe we have all these documents sorted out and ready for your signature," he began and Belinda felt a burden slip from her shoulders.

"You say you have the necessary staff in place?" Mr. Keats questioned.

"Well, not totally," Belinda answered. "We have the kitchen help, extra day staff for the laundry and cleaning, but I still need an assistant for Potter."

"Potter? Oh, yes. She's your housekeeper."

Belinda nodded. "She's done it all herself in the past—but now with so many decisions and the shopping and all the detail work, she will need someone else to supervise the staff. I have interviewed a number of woman, but so far none of them seemed suitable."

"Well, staff can certainly be a problem," he nodded and

spread some sheets before Belinda. "Now, we need your signature on these papers," he continued briskly. "This is to set up the trust fund from which all expenses for the operation of the Manor will be paid."

Belinda nodded and took the pen he offered.

"Now, when you draw funds from this account—" the attorney began.

"Oh, but I won't be the one drawing the funds," Belinda interrupted.

Mr. Keats stopped, a shocked look on his face. "What do you mean?" he asked. "We have set up the funds to be self-perpetuating, so that funds will be available for the continued support of the house."

"Oh, yes," replied Belinda. "That is exactly as I wished, but I won't be the one paying the monthly accounts. I won't be here, you see."

"Not here?"

"I will be leaving for home just as quickly as we can get things settled. I thought I had told you."

The man looked chagrined. "Well, I—I recall some talk. But I thought—I guess I thought you had changed your mind. Nothing has been said about your leaving for some time—"

"Oh, no," Belinda assured him. "I have not changed my mind. I wish to leave as soon as possible."

"I see," said the man, but there was a deep frown across his brow.

"Is that—is that a problem?" asked Belinda.

"Not a problem. We'll have to set things up differently, that's all."

"How—? What will need to change?" Belinda felt her heart sink in frustration.

"Well, a Trust. A Board. I'll need to do some looking into it."

"Oh, dear!" cried Belinda. "I'd so hoped we could finish it all today."

The attorney shook his head. "The way we have it set up now won't do if you are to appoint someone else to administer the estate," he stated simply. "This was arranged for you to have complete charge of the affairs and to administer them accordingly."

He pulled the papers back and stacked them carefully together out of reach of Belinda's pen.

"Will—will it take long?" Belinda asked, her tone agitated.

"That depends. We will need to look into how to set up the administration to best care for the institution and the affairs of the estate. I will need to do some looking into possible alternatives. It would have been much simpler, of course, if you had chosen to run things yourself. But—I'm sure something can be worked out."

Belinda was discouraged as she left the attorney's inner office. There were to be more dealings, more decisions, more frustration.

"Good day, Mr. Willoughby," Belinda said, glancing toward the receptionist as she moved toward the stairs. But she saw he was not alone. A tall man, his back to Belinda was leaning over the desk, discussing some papers.

"Oh, excuse me," Belinda apologized. "I didn't realize—" But she stopped short. There was something familiar about the man. And then he straightened and Belinda saw one sleeve of his suit coat pinned up. The man had only one arm.

Can it possibly be? Belinda's heart gave a sudden lurch. Somehow she knew who it was even before the gentleman turned to look at her.

"Drew?"

The man wheeled sharply, his eyes seeking the face of the young woman before him. "Belinda! Belinda Davis! Why—why—?"

"What are you doing here?" Belinda asked in amazement.

He had taken a step toward her, his hand going out to take hers.

"It *is* you!" he said, shaking his head in wonder. "It really *is* you! I thought I must be dreaming."

"What are you doing here?" Belinda asked again.

"I—I work for this firm," he responded. "And you?"

"You—you work *here*? Why—why haven't I seen you before?

I've been in and out of this office almost daily it seems for—for just *forever*."

"You have?" Drew said in surprise. "You mean—you've been *here*? In Boston?"

"I have been for three years," Belinda informed him.

"I can't believe it! Here we are—in the same city, so—so close to each other and never knowing it. Why didn't someone tell me?"

"I—I had no idea where you were," Belinda explained. "My folks said you were somewhere in the East—training, but they never did say where. I don't know that they even knew."

Drew had still not released her hand. "I can't believe this," he said shaking his head. "We—we have so much catching up to do."

Belinda felt suddenly shy. She withdrew her hand discreetly and fingered her gloves. "Yes," she agreed, the color warming her face, "we do, don't we? Why, I know nothing about—about what you are doing now or your—your—situation," stammered Belinda.

"Are you in a hurry?" asked Drew, and Belinda shook her head.

"Then how about a cup of tea together so we can catch up a bit? I have a few minutes."

"Oh, could we?" Belinda quickly answered. "That would be so nice. I need a friend—someone I can talk to," she said. She was embarrassed to feel tears stinging her eyes.

"Is something wrong?" Drew asked quickly and reached out his arm toward her.

Belinda took one step back and shook her head. "No—no, not really. I've just had too many decisions to make in too short a time. I'm—I'm fine."

Drew nodded, then turned to look at the man at the desk. "Mr. Willoughby, I'm going to be out for half an hour or so. Miss Davis is a friend from home."

Mr. Willoughby, who had missed none of the exchange, nodded silently and turned his eyes back to the paper before him. Drew Simpson took the arm of Miss Davis and led her toward the door. Mr. Willoughby looked up again to watch them go.

"I still can't believe this," Drew was saying. "Imagine, you in Boston."

Drew escorted Belinda to a small tea shop and settled her at a table. "Now," he said, "we don't have nearly enough time, so we will have to talk fast."

Belinda smiled. She no longer felt desperate—or lonely— or shy. She was so glad to see someone from home. She was so glad to see Drew.

"I heard that you visited home a while ago," she commented.

"You were home?"

"Just shortly after you were. I was sorry to hear about your father."

Drew nodded and Belinda saw the grief on his face. "It was a real shock," he said. "To all of us."

"How is your mother?"

"She's—she's fine. She still has Sid, but I'm afraid she never has really adjusted to country living. Still wants Sid to get more education. I've been trying to think of some way—but so far—" Drew shrugged, then changed the subject. "But tell me, what are you doing in Boston?"

They were momentarily interrupted while the waitress set their tea before them. As soon as the girl moved on, Belinda smiled. "Well, it's rather a long story," she said, "but I will save you all the details. My nursing brought me here."

"You nurse in a Boston hospital?"

"No. No, I nursed privately. For an elderly woman but—she is gone now. I'm trying to get the estate settled. That's why I was at the office today."

"I see," said Drew. "So you went right to the top?" he smiled teasingly.

"To the top?"

"Mr. Keats. He's the senior partner."

"I didn't know that," Belinda admitted. "All I know is that settling an estate is an everlasting chore. It seems I've been in and out of the office so often that I should have part ownership."

Drew laughed. "That's how most folks feel by the time they have sorted through legal papers," he admitted.

"But you—what are you doing?" began Belinda. "You said you work there. Doing what?"

Drew smiled again. "Exactly what I was told to do, Belinda Davis. If you remember—practicing law."

"You mean you—you practice law—with them?"

Drew nodded.

"I'm so glad you were able to get your schooling—that you have done your training," she hurried on.

"Finally! Though there were times when I thought I'd never make it, I now am a member of the firm, Keats, Cross and Newman. Though my name doesn't appear on the shingle yet."

"That's wonderful!"

Drew sobered. "It is," he admitted. "And I've never forgotten who made me believe in my dream."

Belinda flushed and toyed with her teacup. "I—we've been out of touch for so long, I guess I don't know much about—about how you've been."

"Nor I you," he admitted. "I've been calling you 'Miss Davis,' but I know it's highly unlikely you haven't married."

Belinda shook her head. "I haven't married," she said simply.

Drew smiled.

There was silence for a bit.

Belinda broke it. "And you?"

Drew shook his head.

It was Belinda's turn to smile.

"How are your folks?" Drew said, lessening the tension at the table.

"Fine. They said you had called. They were pleased. And Luke was—was glad that there is—that you have no—no hard feelings."

"I like your brother Luke," Drew said slowly. "I hadn't realized what a special man he is until I talked to him this last time I was home."

Belinda felt her eyes stinging. "I think he's special, too," she admitted.

They chatted on for some minutes, talking of the hometown they both knew. Belinda didn't want the little visit to end. And then Drew pulled a watch from his vest pocket to check the time. "I hate to say this, but I must get back," he told her, and Belinda couldn't keep the disappointment from her face.

"We won't lose touch again, will we?" he went on. "I mean— now that we know we are both in Boston—"

"Oh, yes. Let's keep in touch," Belinda said a bit too eagerly.

"You have a telephone?"

Belinda nodded and Drew pulled a small pad and pencil from his pocket. Belinda dictated her number.

"I'll be in touch," he promised.

Belinda waited while Drew paid for their refreshments and walked with him back toward the office.

"How will you get home?" he asked her.

"Windsor will soon be here to pick me up," she informed him.

Drew didn't ask who Windsor was and Belinda didn't think to explain.

They had almost reached the law office when Belinda had a sudden inspiration. "Would you—could you—I mean, would it be possible for you to take—to take my—what do you call it—legal—legal case?"

Drew smiled at her fumbling but shook his head. "Mr. Keats, senior partner, is working for you," he reminded her. "I'm just one of the juniors of the firm."

"But you're my friend!" Belinda responded.

"Mr. Keats would say that's all the more reason for me to refrain from acting on your behalf."

"But—but couldn't you just give advice—counsel?"

"I wish I could," said Drew sincerely, reaching to take Belinda's hand. "I do. Really. But it's one of the rules of the firm. No interference of any kind with another attorney's client."

Belinda shrugged. She had so hoped to be able to talk things over with a friend. However, she did understand Drew's sensitive position.

"Very well," she smiled. "I promise not to plague you about my—my legal hassles."

Drew smiled. "Who wants to talk 'legal?' " he asked lightly. "We have too much other catching up to do."

Belinda forgot her worries momentarily and nodded in agreement. "You'd best run—before you get yourself released from your position," she countered.

Drew pressed her hand. "I'll call," he promised, and then Belinda was standing on the sidewalk alone, looking down the street for the carriage and Windsor.

Chapter 18

Friendship

All the way home Belinda marveled at her new discovery. *Drew is in Boston!* she told herself over and over. Drew had not married. Drew was—was all that she remembered him to be, and more. Belinda feared and flushed by turn. *Is it possible,* she finally allowed herself to wonder, *that after all this time Drew might still feel something for me? Is it possible that I still feel something for him?*

The quickening of Belinda's pulse at the very idea made her realize that the latter was more than possible. It was very conceivable. She scolded herself for her silly schoolgirl attitude and tried to calm her feelings.

But each time she determined to corral her churning thoughts, they somehow escaped and returned to Drew. What might have happened if she had discovered three years ago that they shared the same city? She didn't even dare think about it.

Well, I know now, thought Belinda. *So what does the future hold?* Again Belinda flushed and pushed the thought aside. She dared not dwell on it. She would take things one step at a time. God knew whether it was a good idea or not for Drew and her to be more than "friends from back home."

Belinda tried to turn her attention back to the muddle with the estate, but even the ponderous proceedings now failed to dim her spirits.

I must have Drew over for dinner. It'll be so nice to have someone to talk to. To really talk to, she concluded, her eyes bright.

I can hardly wait to write home. Won't Ma and Pa be surprised? Belinda's plans continued. They had no idea Drew was here in Boston. "He is with a good firm," they had said. "Doing well." *But no one knew he was practically my neighbor,* Belinda smiled.

I wonder where he goes to church? she mused. *I must ask him to go with me one day. Maybe we can even—*

Then Belinda again tried to contain her running thoughts. *I'll be so busy getting all the estate's affairs in order that I will have little time for other things,* she reminded herself.

Well, Drew is busy, too, she explained to herself. *But he must have some weekends. At least Sundays. We can go to church together and have dinner and talk,* she reasoned.

But first—first she would have to await his call.

Belinda hoped with all her heart that she wouldn't need to wait too long.

Drew called that evening. Belinda had told herself all afternoon that she could not even hope for a call so soon, but still she found herself straining to hear the ring of the telephone.

When the telephone did ring, it gave her such a start that she nearly fell from her chair. She did drop her needlework and was glad no one was there to see her scrambling to pick it up again.

After all, she scolded herself, *the call could be someone else—* all the while hoping that it wouldn't be.

Belinda tried to look calm and sedate when Windsor announced that she was wanted on the hall telephone. She laid aside her embroidery and walked slowly and with dignity to answer it.

"Hello," she said in what she hoped was an even voice. "Miss Davis here."

"Belinda," his voice quickly came back over the wire. "I was still afraid that I'd dreamed the whole thing."

Belinda laughed softly.

"How are you?" he asked and she had the impression that

it was much more than a pleasantry.

Lonely, she wished she could say. It would be a truthful answer. But instead she said what she felt was expected. "Fine."

"You were a bit down for a while this afternoon, I felt. Have you got it all sorted out now?"

Belinda could have said truthfully that she had sorted out nothing, but that it no longer seemed so important. Instead, she answered, "I'm sure it will all work out. I guess I get too impatient."

"It's hard—waiting," responded Drew. "I'm not good at it either."

There was a moment's silence and then Drew went on with a chuckle. "Which is why I called. I know this is—is presumptuous, but I was wondering if you might be free sometime this weekend."

Belinda could not truthfully say that she had to check her engagement calendar. In fact, she did not even have an engagement calendar, so she didn't play any little game. Instead, she said honestly, openly, "I have no plans—other than church on Sunday."

"Good! Then would you like to take in a concert with me on Saturday night?"

"I'd—I'd like that very much," she replied simply, her heart racing.

"I wish I could ask you for dinner, too, but I have to work. We've a case coming up, and I've been asked to spend Saturday at the office getting ready for it. I'm afraid I will be able to make it only to the concert—this time."

"The concert sounds wonderful," Belinda told him.

"I should have waited until I could make it a proper evening—but—well, I didn't wish to waste any more time. I still can't believe we've lived in the same city for three years without knowing it."

"If you need to work, why don't I meet you at the Opera Hall?" suggested Belinda.

"Oh, but I hate to—" began Drew.

"I wouldn't mind, really. It would be no trouble at all for me to arrange to meet you there."

Drew was still hesitant.

"Really," insisted Belinda.

"You're a great sport," commented Drew. "But it hardly seems like the proper way to treat a young lady."

Belinda laughed. "Well, this young lady doesn't mind a bit. Honestly. I would rather you took a few minutes for a proper meal than to have to quickly dash home and over here to pick me up."

"Thanks, Belinda," Drew finally agreed. "I will meet you there then. Say, eight o'clock. By the east balcony stairs. You know where I'm referring to?"

"Yes. The one near the water fountains."

"Right!"

"Fine. Eight o'clock by the stairs."

Belinda was about to say goodbye when Drew stopped her. "But wait," he said. "If you have one conveyance there, and I another, how will I take you home?"

"Well," she laughed, "I guess I will come home the same way I went. That will save you a trip across town."

"You don't mind?"

"No, I don't mind. It will be nice to enjoy a concert. It's been ages since I have gone. Not since Aunt Virgie—Mrs. Stafford-Smyth—passed away."

"I'll see you there," Drew said and bade her goodbye.

Belinda lingered thoughtfully in the hallway after hanging up the phone. She couldn't believe that after all these years, she was actually going out for an evening with Drew. She too thought it seemed like a dream. A wonderful dream.

Maybe—just maybe this is the reason I could never feel anything for Jackson, or Rand. Maybe, in the back of my mind, I have always felt like my heart—that I sort of—belonged to Drew.

She blushed at the thought and hurried in to snatch up her needlework. But she could not concentrate. Eventually she rang for Potter.

"I believe I'll make an early night of it, Potter," she explained. "Don't bother with tea later."

Potter nodded, then asked with concern, "You aren't comin' down with somethin' are you, miss?"

"Oh, no. No. Nothing like that. It's been a long day. The attorney still has us tied up in legal wrangling. I guess I feel a bit edgy."

Potter still looked worried.

"It'll all sort itself out, I'm sure," Belinda smiled.

"I was thinking of *you*, miss—not the house. You look rather flushed," Potter responded, and Belinda was surprised. The older woman sounded so genuinely concerned.

"I'm fine. Really," she insisted, knowing why her cheeks were rosy. The housekeeper nodded and turned to leave.

"And, Potter," Belinda called, "on Saturday night I would like dinner a bit earlier. I'll be going out. Could you inform Cook, please?"

Potter nodded, her eyes brightening with unasked questions. "Very well, miss. What time?"

"Around six, I should think."

Potter nodded again.

"Good night, then," said Belinda, giving the matronly woman a smile.

"Sleep well, miss," replied Potter and Belinda smiled again as the woman left the room. She planned to do just that.

But she didn't. Her mind was far too busy with many things, not the least of which were mental pictures and imaginary conversations with an old friend by the name of Drew Simpson.

Belinda was in a tizzy on Saturday. She was so restless that she couldn't settle down to any of her appointed tasks. She felt annoyed with herself. "After all, it's just a concert with an old friend," she told herself. But try as she might her heart would not accept the reasoning of her mind. She finally fled to the gardens and Thomas for some kind of diversion.

Thomas was busy cleaning the flower beds of debris and fallen leaves. The fall flowers were the only ones blooming now. Thomas always liked to have everything nice and tidy long before the winter storms visited the Manor property.

"Your mums are beautiful, Thomas," Belinda said, bringing a smile to the old man's face.

"It will soon be time to work with the bulbs," stated Thomas.

"Seems every yeah speeds by just a little fastah."

Belinda nodded, though she herself had felt that this year was particularly slow.

"Just bloom and it's time to cut them back," Thomas was saying gloomily. "The season flies by so fast you scarcely get to enjoy them." Belinda thought she knew how the old man felt.

She lingered for a few minutes, patted the head of the docile McIntyre, and then wandered off down the path. There were still plenty of pretty things to see. She would miss the gardens. Probably even more than she would miss the house with all its pretty things.

Belinda managed to tick a few more minutes from her day as she dallied, but soon she could endure no more wanderings and hastened back to the house to study the clock again.

At last she allowed herself to retire to her room to choose her dress for the evening. She pulled gown after gown from the closet and studied them and then hung them back. Drew might judge some of her silks and satins too elaborate for a country girl. On the other hand, she didn't want to look plain and dowdy either. She looked at another gown, studied that one and debated it all over again. It did serve to fill in a few more minutes of the long day.

At last Belinda selected a green gown with classic lines. *It has style without being fussy,* she reasoned. *With some simple jewelry and my hair fixed, I'll fit in nicely with the concert crowd and be well dressed without being "showy."* Belinda nodded in satisfaction as she laid the dress on her bed and prepared for a bath.

She had not called Ella to help with grooming preparations for some time, but she allowed herself the luxury of ringing Ella now—partly because she needed someone to talk to. She feared she might explode if she didn't have some way to release a little of her pent-up excitement.

Ella responded immediately to the ring. "Yes, miss?"

"Would you draw me a bath please, Ella?" Belinda requested. "The jasmine scent, I believe. And then I would like you to fix my hair. I am attending the concert tonight with an old friend."

Belinda saw the flutter of curiosity and excitement in Ella's eyes, but the girl avoided asking the questions she so obviously would have liked to ask. "Yes, miss." she said again and went to comply.

"It's been a long time since you've been to a concert, miss," Ella dared to say as she came out of the bathroom.

"Yes," agreed Belinda. "A very long time."

She pinned her hair up so that it wouldn't get wet. "I'm quite looking forward to it."

Ella nodded, a smile on her lips. It was obvious that Belinda was flushed with excitement.

Then Ella became unforgivably bold. "Is your friend visiting in town?" she asked.

"No."

"She lives here?"

"He," corrected Belinda. "He."

"Oh," responded Ella, pleased with the information she had pulled from her young mistress, "I thought maybe it was someone from your hometown."

Belinda could not hide the excitement in her voice. "Oh, he is. But he's in Boston now. He has been here for years, and I didn't even know until the other day. He is an attorney—with the same firm that has been doing my legal work. Can you imagine? Neither of us knew that the other was in the city. We just happened to meet last Thursday."

By now Ella was smiling broadly. She hadn't dared to hope for so much information. "Why, that's smashing, miss," she enthused. "No wonder you're excited—going to the concert—and with an old friend. How nice!"

Belinda agreed.

"Your bath is ready now, miss," Ella told her. "I'll be back in twenty minutes to do your hair."

The truth was Ella could hardly wait to share her exciting news with Sarah.

Chapter 19

The Concert

Drew was already waiting by the stairs when Belinda found her way through the crowded lobby. He eagerly moved to greet her and offered her his arm as he led her toward their seats. "You make that dress look lovely," he whispered for her ears only.

Belinda smiled at the compliment.

"How was your day?" she asked him.

"Long. But profitable," he answered. "I did manage to get a lot done—though the day seemed to do a lot of dragging."

Belinda certainly agreed, though she did not say so.

"Do you come here often?" Belinda asked as they were seated.

"Oh, no. Not nearly as often as I'd like. At first I was much too busy studying. And besides I had to work when I wasn't in class in order to pay my way through school. I didn't have the money or the time to spend in such places as this."

Belinda admired his frankness.

"How long have you been with Keats, Cross and Newman?" she asked.

"About a year." He chuckled. "So now I've finally earned enough to afford an occasional treat. I decided about six months ago that I should soak up a bit of culture. So I went—once."

Belinda's face showed her bewilderment. "Didn't you enjoy it?" she asked.

161

"The music, yes. But I just didn't enjoy going alone."

Belinda nodded. "I feel the same way," she admitted. "I have not even gone once since Aunt Virgie died."

"Well, now we have each other's company," Drew said with a smile. "Shall we come every week?"

Belinda smiled back. She wasn't sure if Drew really was expecting an answer or was just teasing.

The orchestra began to warm up and it became difficult to talk. Drew leaned closer and whispered, "This is the one part of the concert I would gladly forego. Makes one wonder how such a horrid noise could ever all come together to make any kind of music."

Belinda chuckled at his little joke, feeling close and contented. It was so nice to be with a friend.

The evening was a total delight to Belinda. Every piece that was played was a "favorite." At least that was how the music affected her. Drew seemed to feel the same way. They nodded to one another, whispered little comments now and then and totally enjoyed their time spent together.

At the break they left their seats and went for a cold drink. They stood in a shadowed recess of the main hall and sipped lemonade punch and made delightful small talk, getting to know each other all over again. Then they joined the crowd drifting back to their seats for the second half of the performance.

"We must do this again," Drew whispered as the last applause was fading away, and Belinda nodded dreamily.

"I wish I could escort you home," he continued and Belinda earnestly wished he could too. It was all she could do to keep from suggesting that she send Windsor on home alone and have Drew drive her. But common sense prevailed. After all, it was late and Drew must be very weary.

"Would you be interested in coming to church with me tomorrow?" she asked instead and Drew's eyes lit up.

"I'd love to," he agreed.

"Fine. The service is at ten o'clock. The church is on First and Maple. I'll meet you there and then you can come to dinner."

"I would like that, very much," he returned with enthusiasm.

They moved through the crowded foyer and made their way toward the street.

"Windsor said he'd wait near that streetlight," Belinda informed Drew and he steered her in that direction.

Windsor was waiting as he promised and there seemed to be no reason to linger. So Belinda bid Drew good night and thanked him again for the concert.

"Until tomorrow at ten," he said softly and her heart gave a joyful skip. And then Windsor was clucking to the horses and they were on their way, moving briskly through the city streets.

Belinda had quite a time getting to sleep that night. She went over and over each portion of the wonderful evening. She reviewed each part of the conversation, each selection of the orchestra, each moment of their time together—and then she reminded herself that she must get some sleep if she was going to be at her best the next morning. Even so she had a most difficult time stilling her spinning brain and her beating heart.

The next morning Belinda hummed as she dressed in her most becoming suit and pinned her feather-draped hat on shiny curls. It was a beautiful fall morning, and she looked forward to her drive to church. She had considered walking, but if the wind should arise it could blow her hair and the feathers on her hat and she would get to church breathless and concerned. So she advised Windsor to bring the carriage as usual.

Drew was waiting on the church steps when she arrived and she greeted him warmly and led the way into the large sanctuary.

"This is huge," Drew whispered. "Are you sure you won't get us lost?"

Belinda smiled.

"I've never been in such a big church," he commented.

"Where do you attend?" she asked him.

"A little mission—right downtown. You'll have to come with me sometime."

"I'd like that," Belinda replied. They were ushered into a pew and prepared themselves for the morning worship.

Belinda was pleased to hear Drew beside her, singing the familiar hymns. He had a pleasant voice and was not afraid to sing out heartily. Most of the congregation in the big church were rather timid about singing.

The minister's sermon was good—correct in content and flawless in delivery.

The two were greeted at the door as they left the sanctuary and a few of the parishoners nodded Belinda's way. After all, she had been a faithful part of this church for three years.

"How did you arrive?" Belinda asked Drew.

"I hired a carriage," he answered simply.

"You didn't ask the driver to wait, did you?"

"No. I paid him and sent him on his way."

"Good," she responded. "Windsor has been sent along home, too."

"You're going to walk?" teased Drew. "In your Sunday finery?"

"It's only a short distance," Belinda told him. "It will help me appreciate my dinner."

Drew fell into step beside her. "This is a very nice part of town," he commented as he looked about them. "Your former employer must have been a lady of means."

Belinda nodded. She had told Drew very little about Mrs. Stafford-Smyth. "Did I tell you how I met her?" asked Belinda. "No, I thought not. Well, she was traveling. She loved to travel. Went all the way to San Francisco—'just to see it,' she said. She traveled out by train and on her way home she was taken ill—at our town. They brought her to Luke. She was really very sick. Had suffered a stroke. We didn't know for days if she would make it. But she did. Gradually. When she was well enough to travel on home, she asked me to accompany her. I did because I was—well, bored, I guess, and had never seen anything but our little town."

"So you came to Boston," said Drew. "Now I remember, Luke told me briefly of your out-of-town patient. I hadn't realized that you had been with her all this time. You stayed on with her then?"

"I did. I intended to accompany her here and then return again. But she wanted me to stay on and I agreed. I always thought I would stay just a bit longer because she needed me. She was so lonely."

"Didn't she have family?"

"Two grandsons. But they both live in Paris. Their mother was French. Aunt Virgie kept hoping and praying that they would decide to return to America—but it didn't work that way. They both married French girls and settled down over there."

"So now she is gone—and you are still here?"

Belinda nodded.

"And you have the affairs of the estate to handle—rather than the grandsons?"

Belinda could tell that Drew thought the matter rather strange. It would seem so to anyone.

"She left the boys each a sizable amount of money," Belinda said.

"And—" Drew prompted.

"She was a very generous lady. She left her staff each part of the estate as well."

Drew nodded. "And you have to wait for all the estate to be put in order?"

"Right," she responded with a sigh. "I was so in hopes that it would be cared for by now—but it all takes so much time. We still need to—" Belinda caught herself. "But I promised I wouldn't discuss that, didn't I? Firm rules. This is Mr. Keat's affair."

Drew smiled.

They walked along in silence and then Belinda led the way down the long driveway toward the magnificently appointed home.

Drew's eyes widened. "You're not telling me that this is home, are you?" he asked.

"This is Marshall Manor," announced Belinda. "And I know just how you feel. I felt that way myself the first time I saw it."

"I believe it," Drew murmured, drawing in a breath. "I've

never seen a house like this one in my entire life. No wonder it is taking an age to settle the estate."

"I suppose that has something to do with it," she admitted and led the way through the front door to the wide entrance hall. Windsor was waiting to take the gentleman's hat and relieve Belinda of her parasol.

"Come," Belinda said to Drew. "I'll show you where you can freshen up. Dinner will be served in a few minutes."

Drew was studying the paintings in the entrance when Belinda came back down the stairs from her room. "I've never seen such grandeur," he admitted. "I can't imagine what it must be like to live here."

Belinda wrinkled her nose. "I must admit to being a bit spoiled," she confessed. "I found it most difficult to go back to farmyard plumbing on my last trip home."

Drew laughed. "I should think so," he agreed.

Windsor announced dinner and Belinda led the way to the dining room. The table was a large one to be set with just two places, and Drew mentioned the fact after he had seated Belinda.

"It looks good today," she said soberly. "Usually it only has one."

"You eat in here—alone?" Drew asked as the first course was served.

Belinda nodded.

"Couldn't you just—isn't there a less formal, smaller table somewhere?"

"Off the kitchen," smiled Belinda.

"Well, couldn't you—well, use it?"

Belinda laughed softly. "That does not seem appropriate to the staff," she informed him. "They would be uncomfortable if I did such a thing."

"But—but I thought you *were* staff," Drew countered.

Belinda laughed heartily. "I was. It was most strange— Aunt Virgie insisted that I eat with her. She was just lonely, I think, and I was the only staff member who hadn't been brought up 'by the rules,' so to speak. So when she expected me to be at the table, I didn't have the sense to object. At first the other household staff was scandalized by it."

"But now she is gone and you are still at the table," observed Drew.

"That's the strange part. Now they would be equally scandalized if I were to suggest eating near the kitchen with them."

"So you always eat here—alone?"

"Oh, no. Not always. Sometimes I ask for my meal in the north parlor on a tray. Or in my room. But *never* in the dining hall off the kitchen."

After asking God's blessing on the food, they began to eat.

"Well, I must say, it's the most delicious food I've tasted for quite some time," Drew admitted.

"Oh, Cook is most proud of her culinary skills," stated Belinda.

Drew was still shaking his head. Then he looked directly at Belinda. "I have to admit," he said simply, "you do look perfectly at home here."

Belinda smiled. "I suppose I've had some practice," she responded. "I felt very much out of my element at first. Especially when Aunt Virgie would entertain. She always had guests her own age and the conversation was from another world than the one I'd known."

Drew smiled. "I can see the problem," he admitted.

"Shall we have coffee and dessert on the veranda?" Belinda asked later. "Thomas does a wonderful job on the gardens. The fall flowers are still very pretty, but I'm afraid we might not be able to enjoy them for long. Thomas says the seasons come and go so quickly that the flowers scarcely have a chance to bloom."

Drew nodded and Belinda rang for Windsor.

"We'll have our coffee and dessert on the veranda, Windsor," she informed the butler and fell into step beside Drew.

Drew was just as overwhelmed by the gardens as he had been by the house.

"Thomas is always out here working in them," Belinda informed him. "Every day but Sunday. Even in the rain. In the winter he putters in his greenhouse getting plants ready for the next year's planting."

"Well, he is certainly skilled," Drew commented. "This is the prettiest setting I've ever seen."

"I love the gardens—almost as much as old Thomas does," Belinda said.

"I just can't imagine anyone living like this," Drew observed.

"You get used to it," Belinda replied with a slight shrug.

" 'Used to it,' " laughed Drew. "Listen to you. Used to it. As if it were a comfortable old shoe or something."

Belinda joined him in laughter. Windsor brought the dessert and coffee. "I'll pour, Windsor," Belinda offered. "That will be all, thank you."

Drew watched her carefully but made no comment. She did appear to be very much at home issuing orders and living in elegant style. Drew stirred uneasily.

Looking about him at the magnificent home, he pondered, "Seems a shame to have it all pass on to someone else. Someone who might not love it in the way your former employer did."

"That's why I don't want it sold," Belinda agreed. "I just couldn't let Aunt Virgie's house be taken over by strangers."

Drew looked surprised. "It won't be sold? But I thought you said you were busy settling the estate."

"Oh, yes. I am."

"Doesn't it have to be sold to give each of the heirs the portion mentioned in the will? You said—"

"Oh, the specifics mentioned in the will were quite apart from the house," Belinda informed Drew. "In fact, all that has been taken care of. That wasn't the difficult part."

Drew looked more puzzled.

"The problem has been setting things up for the house— and grounds. I don't want things to deteriorate. It takes a good deal of planning to maintain such a place."

"You have to do all of that?" he asked astonished.

"Oh, yes," responded Belinda simply. "Aunt Virgie left it all to me."

Chapter 20

The Disappointment

Belinda had no idea the effect her words would have on Drew. The impact of the simple statement took the wind from him as forcibly as the long ago fall from Copper had taken it from Belinda. Belinda's wealth put an impossible barrier between her and a struggling young attorney.

Belinda was still speaking. "It's been a great frustration," she said. "We have gone round and round trying to get things set up properly."

Drew nodded, dumbly.

"But finally things seem to be drawing to a close. At least that's what Mr. Keats says. I have another appointment with him next Wednesday."

Drew nodded again. He still had not found his voice.

"Mrs. Stafford-Smyth must have thought a great deal of you," he managed at last.

For a moment Belinda did not comment and when she did, she had tears in her eyes. "We were more like family than employer and employee," she admitted. "She was so good to me. I miss her very much."

Drew would have liked to move forward to comfort Belinda, but he held back.

Belinda was unaware of Drew's hesitation.

"She always missed her grandsons so much," she explained, "but she knew they would never move here to America—not even for this beautiful home. So she did what she could to keep it like this." Belinda looked about her and waved her hand. "She gave it to me. She knew I would do all I could to keep it just as it is—as much as possible."

Drew nodded, his pain still unnoticed by Belinda.

"It seems like—like a lot of house for one small woman," Drew said with a sigh, looking around into the large dining room.

"Exactly," agreed Belinda. "That's why I've decided to share it."

"Share it?"

"With the elderly. We are planning to invite ten older people—people who do not have homes or families—to live here."

Drew's eyes widened in surprise.

"So you see," laughed Belinda merrily, "the dining room table will no longer need to be set for one."

Drew managed a smile. "Doesn't it—doesn't it bother you—having all those people—strangers—moving into your beautiful home?" he asked.

"Oh, no," Belinda shook her head firmly. "It really seems the only way to do it."

"You mean—you—you need the income for the upkeep?" he finally asked with difficulty.

"Oh, no. Nothing like that. There's plenty of money for that. The new boarders won't be charged anything. They will be guests—for as long as they wish to live here."

Drew shook his head. "I've never heard of an arrangement like that," he said to Belinda.

"I guess others haven't either. That's what makes it so difficult to set it up. Even Mr. Keats is hard-put knowing how to go about it."

"I see," said Drew. The day seemed to have lost its joy. Drew set aside his cup and stood to his feet.

"Well, I guess I shouldn't outstay my welcome," he murmured.

"Your welcome? Oh, you could never do that," responded Belinda. "Come, let me show you the rest of the house."

Drew politely followed Belinda on the guided tour. The more

he saw, the more dejected he became. Belinda could sense it, but she had no idea why he was bothered.

"You'll come again?" she asked anxiously when he took his leave.

Drew didn't answer her question directly. "Don't forget you promised to come to the mission with me," he reminded Belinda.

"Oh, I'd love to," she responded excitedly and Drew's countenance lifted for a moment. But then Belinda added, "I might find some elderly people there who need this home."

Drew, disappointed, nodded solemnly and turned to go.

"But how are you getting home?" Belinda asked him.

"Oh, I'll find a carriage," he said, shrugging his shoulders.

"Nonsense," insisted Belinda, "Windsor will drive you."

Drew began to argue but Belinda had quite made up her mind.

"I'll even ride along—if you don't mind," she said with a smile, and Drew agreed helplessly.

Belinda knew nothing of the discouraging thoughts racing through the mind of her companion since he had discovered her true situation—that Belinda was a very wealthy woman. Instead, she thought about the wonder of their finding each other in Boston. She revelled in the fact that they were able to enjoy one another's company. She relived the moments spent together and looked forward to many such happy times in the future.

And then Belinda thought of her plans for going home, and her heart sank within her. It was obvious to her that Drew planned to stay on in Boston. He had a promising future with an established law firm. He would be foolish to give up all that for—for a hometown girl.

Belinda suddenly shivered. There seemed to be more than a hint of fall in the air. A strange silence fell between the two travelers.

"I have discovered several ways that we can go," Mr. Keats began on Belinda's next visit. "But in each case it will involve setting up a trust and administrators."

Belinda nodded.

"The main issue is what kind of trust you wish to set up."

"What choices do I have?" asked Belinda.

"Well, we could set it up under the city administration. They do have a concern committee to care for the homeless. Your proposal might fit into their program."

Belinda considered that.

"Or," went on Mr. Keats, "we could set it up under a church. They have contacts with the needy and could administer it as they see fit."

Belinda spent another period of time thinking of that possibility.

"Or," continued the attorney, "we could set it up independently. A board quite apart from either of those. Self-governed and self-controlled."

Belinda thought some more. "I favor that idea," she finally said.

The man nodded. "One needs to be very careful about choosing the administrators," he cautioned.

"How about an attorney, a banker, a member from the city and a church official?" suggested Belinda timidly.

The man nodded. "Good choices," he said, looking surprised. "I would recommend a few more."

"Would you serve on my board?" Belinda dared to ask.

Mr. Keats was obviously flattered. "Well, I—I would be honored," he replied.

Belinda felt that they had finally made a significant step. The rest of the appointment time was spent in discussing possible board members; and when Belinda left, Mr. Keats had her instructions to make the contacts.

Belinda was hoping she might run into Drew. She wanted to share her good news. And then she remembered that her good news was also bad news—at least to her way of thinking. Once the Manor affairs were settled, she would have no reason to linger in Boston. She would be saying goodbye to Drew again—and this time there was little likelihood that their paths would cross.

I could stay right here and run the Manor, Belinda thought. *No one would ask me to leave.*

But in her heart Belinda knew that was out of the question. She needed, desperately needed, to touch base with her roots again—to discover the real Belinda Davis. She had been living in another world—in many ways a false world—for too long. She didn't belong there and she wasn't even happy in that life-style. She hadn't been raised to be a parlor pansy in some magnificent Boston home. She was a simple person at heart. She had learned from her parents to think of others—to seek direction from God as to how she could serve.

I definitely have to go home. And Drew will be staying on in Boston. There's no use encouraging anything more than friendship. At least I will say my farewell with some kind of dignity, she determined.

In spite of the resolves made on both sides, Drew continued to call Belinda for engagements, and she continued to say yes to each invitation. They attended Drew's small mission church, as previously planned. Belinda was enthralled. It reminded her so much of the small community church back home. The people were openly friendly, the singing so enthusiastic, and the Gospel presented in such a simple but easy-to-understand fashion. Belinda felt right at home. She told Drew her impressions and he nodded and smiled, pleased that she had enjoyed the church.

She didn't find any elderly in need, though she did ask Drew to keep his eyes and ears open.

They attended another concert, enjoyed a Saturday picnic at the park, visited some local museums, and took long walks. And during the time they spent together they were telling themselves that they were enjoying a simple friendship—nothing more—because the circumstances would not allow for anything else. But within each heart, the feelings were growing more and more intense.

Things can't drag on like this, Belinda decided as the first snowfall of the year swirled about the Manor. *I must get things settled here once and for all and be off for home.*

She spent the morning on the telephone, and by the time she was through, five residents had been secured for the Manor.

The big house would soon be filled with activity.

I still need help for Mrs. Potter, Belinda reminded herself. *Mrs. Simpson!* she thought suddenly in a flash of inspiration. *Drew would be happy to have his mother here,* Belinda reasoned. *She could help in the house and Sid could go to school.* It seemed like a fine plan to Belinda and she couldn't wait to discuss it with Drew.

When he phoned that evening, Belinda was quick to put her idea to him. At first he seemed a bit hesitant, but the more Belinda talked the more he seemed to agree.

"Do you think she would consider it?" Belinda asked.

"I'm sure she would," Drew admitted. "She has wanted to return to the city for a long time."

"But would she mind—mind working with Mrs. Potter?"

"Mother was never afraid of hard work," Drew answered. He thought for a moment and then said, "We might even be able to find something for Sid."

"I thought he should be in school," Belinda told Drew. "He could help part time here at the Manor with some of the extra chores, and take classes at one of the local universities."

"You have thought of everything, haven't you?" Drew chuckled.

"You think it will work then?" asked Belinda.

"I think Mother would be delighted," Drew said honestly.

So Belinda sent off a letter with two train tickets and an advance of cash enclosed and held her breath until she received the reply. Mrs. Simpson and Sid would be arriving on the twenty-fifth of November. With a great feeling of excitement she called Drew.

It was a cold, wintry day when Belinda prepared to meet the incoming train. She had first thought she would send Windsor on his own but then realized the Simpsons might be more comfortable being met by someone they knew. Drew had offered to meet the train, but Belinda insisted she had more time for that than he did. "Come in the morning to see them," she invited.

Belinda was glad she had decided to meet the Simpsons

when they arrived instead of sending Windsor. Both mother and son seemed uncomfortable and nervous. Windsor saw to the baggage and Belinda led the two travelers to the waiting carriage.

"It's cold tonight," she told them. "Be sure to wrap the blankets around you." She passed them two of the heavy blankets Windsor had placed in the carriage and proceeded to bundle herself carefully in her own blanket. The two passengers followed her lead.

She chatted about their hometown and drew bits of information from Sid. He had grown up since Belinda had last seen him, and she was impressed. He had turned out to be a fine-looking young man. Mrs. Simpson was her usual quiet self, although she did answer Belinda's questions.

When they arrived at the Manor, both of the tired travelers seemed to come to life in fascination with their new abode. Even Mrs. Simpson made some comments.

Belinda knew that the rules had now changed. Potter was the administrator of the Manor and as such would need to make all the decisions concerning the staff. And the Simpsons were *staff*, even though Belinda would like to have treated them as her guests. So Belinda, wisely, turned the two weary newcomers over to Potter, knowing that they would be served refreshments and shown to their rooms.

Tiredly, Belinda climbed the stairs to her own rooms. She was anxious for a hot bath and a good rest. Drew would be coming in the morning to greet his mother and brother. Belinda could foresee another heart-wrenching day—the emotional trap to keep her here in Boston, at odds with her desire to return to her roots.

Chapter 21

Final Preparations

Belinda had hoped to have all the arrangements concerning the Manor finished by Christmastime, but as time went by she began to realize that it would be impossible. She eventually gave up on the idea and started to make plans for Christmas in Boston.

Perhaps it is better this way, she thought. *Potter may need my help during her first Christmas as administrator.* But Belinda secretly wondered if another reason for staying on was to delay saying farewell to Drew.

Mrs. Simpson settled quickly and efficiently into her role as housekeeper. She had several staff under her, including cleaning and laundry services. There would be plenty to do once the Manor had all its residents in place.

On December 6 the first two elderly occupants moved in. Mrs. Simpson had their rooms all ready for them in accordance with Potter's instructions, and the two ladies were settled and then given a grand tour of the house.

One of the new guests had been a piano teacher in the past, and she was delighted to find a music room and an instrument. The other was very impressed with the library. Belinda found the two delightful and wished she could ask each one for the complete story of her life.

They deserve their privacy, she reminded herself. *They will tell what they wish when they wish.*

And so it happened. Little by little bits of information came to life as the ladies sat in the north parlor at teatime or before the open fire with their handwork or a book.

Mrs. Bailey was a widow. At one time she, with her husband and three children, lived in a modest home on Boston's south side. Her husband was a drayman until a back injury ended his working days. Mrs. Bailey took on the support of the family by taking in laundry, selling baked goods, and sewing. Then even worse tragedy struck. The youngest child fell into the Charles River and the older one tried to save him. Both children drowned. A number of years later, tuberculosis took the life of their remaining daughter. Then the woman's crippled husband passed away as well.

Belinda found it hard to believe that one person could endure so much tragedy. Yet the woman was still able to smile and to thank God for seeing her through all the difficulties. "And now the Lord has given me time to read and a whole library full of books," she rejoiced, waving a favorite title.

The second woman, Miss Mitton, had never married and had taught piano for many years to support herself. But when the number of students dwindled, she had to move from her neat little apartment to a shoddy tenement in the poorest section of town. The move made her bitter and cynical. "Why should one in her position and education be forced to live in such abject poverty?" she lamented. Struggling against her situation, her burden grew even greater.

With a feeling of justice finally being given her, Miss Mitton took up her residence at the Manor. She held her chin high to let it be known that she really belonged in this class. Though the woman had never lived in such surroundings in her entire life, she was accepted without judgment. Belinda smiled and humored her. She felt sorry for the little woman who tried so hard to be something she was not.

"I should not be forced to accept charity," Mrs. Mitton insisted one day as she struggled to hold her teacup daintily in shaky hands. "Fate has handed me some evil turns—but I really was born and bred in gentility."

"You were very blessed," Belinda said softly. "Like many of

us here, I was not. My home was ordinary, though most adequate. We had love and understanding and proper food and clothing. I guess I learned early that velvets and porcelains are not what constitute a 'good' life.

"But please, let us make one thing clear from the beginning. No one at Marshall Manor is accepting charity. This is *home* for you and each resident. We have invited you to live with us because we want you here. A house is lonely if it does not have family. We are now a family."

Miss Mitton's chin lifted a bit higher, but Mrs. Bailey brushed tears from her eyes.

Belinda made another trip to see Mr. Keats, hoping that things were finally in order. He met her at the door with a broad grin. She took that as a good omen.

"Things have progressed satisfactorily?" she asked.

"Yes, quite," he answered, still beaming at his achievement. "Your board is all in order. They've had their first meeting and have established their directives. The banker and I will handle the paying of accounts—with board approval, of course. The minister and two of the other board members will see to finding the residents as needed. By Christmas the Manor should be filled, and you should be free to carry on with your other plans—whatever they might be."

Belinda nodded. The long process was finally drawing to a close.

"I've been thinking," she said. "It would be nice to have a spiritual counselor—a chaplain—for the home."

The attorney looked over his glasses. "A chaplain?" he said.

"Yes," faltered Belinda, feeling somewhat on the defensive. "To lead the daily devotional times and Sunday services should the residents be unable to go out."

"Have the residents requested a chaplain?"

"No-o."

"Perhaps they are not quite so—so religious as you seem to be." stated the attorney frankly.

"But they haven't requested *anything*," defended Belinda. "They haven't moved into the Manor demanding this or that. But we do need to care for their needs—physical and spiritual."

"I see," said the lawyer, but Belinda wondered if he really did. Perhaps the attorney was not the one she should be speaking to concerning a chaplain for the Manor, she decided. *Very well,* she silently conceded. *I'll talk to God about the chaplain.* To Mr. Keats she said, "We do need a physician. We are dealing with the elderly, and it is common for one ailment or another to need immediate care."

The man nodded. "Do you mean a resident physician?" he asked her.

"Oh, no, no. But one should be on call. And should drop by regularly."

"I think we can arrange that with no problem. I will look into it right away."

Belinda smiled her thanks.

"But perhaps it would be wise to have a nurse actually in residence," the attorney went on. "She could care for small problems and call the doctor as needed."

Belinda thought it did sound reasonable.

"I understand that you are—were a nurse," the man said hesitantly; "but of course with your position changed so dramatically, I'm sure you wouldn't be interested in such a position. However, it should help you in securing a qualified person."

Belinda knew the man considered her a wealthy woman, thanks to Mrs. Stafford-Smyth's inheritance. He still hadn't seemed to realize that she was placing it in the hands of others and would not be drawing from it.

"It's—it's not that," Belinda stammered. "It's just that I plan to go home."

"Oh, yes," the man said with a nod of his head, but she knew he was still puzzled.

"But I'll think about the situation as you have suggested," Belinda agreed.

All the way home Belinda wrestled with her thoughts. *Is a nurse really needed? Am I needed? Is this God's way of showing me that I should—that I can stay on in Boston? Might there be good reason to think that—that Drew and I could make a life together after all?*

Belinda felt her cheeks flushing. She did care deeply for Drew, she admitted to herself frankly. But she also realized that he had really given her no reason to foster such hopes and dreams. He had been kind and caring, had seemed to enjoy her company, but he had never said or done anything to make Belinda think he might love her.

Belinda shoved aside her dreams and tried to still her pounding heart. It would be wrong, a great mistake, for her to change her plans based only on hopes that Drew would someday ask her to marry him, she knew. That would be a very awkward situation in which to place herself. And also an awkward situation in which to place Drew. *No,* she decided, *I will not build false dreams that might never come to be.*

I must look for a nurse, she decided resolutely, and with determination she set out to find the proper person.

On December 10 three more residents moved into the Manor. Mr. Rudgers was a tall, thin man with an untidy mustache and a twinkle in his eyes. Belinda took to him immediately. She could well imagine that his humor was going to keep things lively. His eyes fastened on Miss Mitton almost immediately, and Belinda wasn't sure if he had picked her as a likely target for his good-natured jokes or because there was something in the woman that attracted him. Belinda was sure only time would reveal his real reason.

Mr. Lewis, wizened and bent from illness or the heavy burden of life itself, had no twinkle in his eyes, only sorrow. But he asked for little, accepted all with appreciation, and contented himself with a chair in the corner. Belinda hoped that life in the Manor would soon erase some of the pain from his eyes.

Mrs. Gibbons was wiry and talkative. She fluttered about here and there, asking questions. And it turned out that the answers were never confidential information. Mrs. Gibbons was very hard of hearing. "Aye?" she would question, a hand cupped to her ear. "I didn't catch thet." But it was a sure thing that everyone else in the room had "caught" it. Belinda felt that with Mrs. Gibbons to prompt and prod, everyone would be acquainted in no time at all.

Three more guests moved in the week before Christmas. The total was now five women and three men. And on December 21, a marvelous thing happened. A retired minister and his wife came to the Manor. Their home had been destroyed by fire and they had no means to rebuild. Belinda sorrowed for their loss, but she felt the couple was God's answer to her prayers.

The gentle old man smiled as Belinda asked him about becoming the spiritual director for the residents.

"God be praised, Nettie," he said, addressing his silver-haired helpmate of many years. "He has given us a home *and* a place of service—not a shelf on which to sit."

Tears traced a path down the woman's softly wrinkled cheeks. "God be praised," she echoed.

Belinda rejoiced right along with them. It was almost Christmas, and with the assigning of the elderly couple to Mrs. Stafford-Smyth's former rooms, the Manor residents were all in place.

"Potter, you are in complete charge here," Belinda informed the administrator. "I don't wish to interfere—but if there is any way that I can help you with your plans for our first Christmas all together, I would be delighted."

Potter smiled. "I'd appreciate that, miss," she acknowledged. "It has been troubling me some."

So the two of them sat down and plotted out the plans for the Christmas celebration. The menu was left in the capable hands of Cook and her staff.

With the help of Sid, Windsor set up a tree in the parlor and decorated the hall with garlands and boughs. Belinda did the shopping, choosing a simple gift for each Manor resident. In future years they could exchange names at Christmas and buy small gifts from their allotted monthly funds.

The long dining room table sparkled with the good china and stemware, and the silver candlesticks held decorated candles. Belinda looked at the table, remembering Christmases past, and concluded that the day would be a special one indeed.

The fact that Drew was coming made the day even more special. This at first had posed a problem for Belinda. All the staff would be having their dinner in the room off the kitchen. That would mean that Mrs. Simpson and Sid would be eating there. *I can hardly ask Drew to eat in the dining room while his mother sits with the staff in a back room,* Belinda sighed.

But a sudden thought made her brighten quickly. She was no longer the mistress of the Manor. There was no reason why she couldn't appoint herself a spot at the staff table as well. Feeling much better, she went about decorating the staff table. She used good linen from the linen closet, set the table up with china plates, found another set of candlesticks and arranged small pine boughs and cones. It looked very festive, and Belinda was pleased with the results.

When Christmas Eve arrived, all was in readiness. The Manor was filled with residents—only Belinda's personal rooms had not been assigned. Belinda still hoped she could turn over her rooms to a resident nurse, but in spite of her inquiries, she had not yet been able to find one.

Maybe it's foolish to even hope for such a thing, she told herself. *I might happen upon a retired minister, but I'm sure I'll not find a retired nurse. We may need to content ourselves with doctors who are willing to make house calls.*

The Manor Board was established, the funds available for the continued support of the home, and physicians had been found who were willing to serve the residents of the Manor. Belinda smiled softly to herself. She thought of the long, long months of planning and preparation. Deep within, she felt that Mrs. Stafford-Smyth would approve of what she had done.

If only— she thought. *If only I had a resident nurse, then everything would be properly in place by Christmas.*

Belinda took one more glance around. Things did look nice. So homey. And it felt homey, too.

From the music room came the sound of Miss Mitton playing some Christmas carols. Occasionally the teasing voice of Mr. Rudgers reached Belinda. *He's at it again, pestering Miss Mitton with his jokes and comments,* she thought wryly. But over the few days they had shared the big house, things had changed.

Miss Mitton now giggled in response.

From the north parlor came animated chatter, with an occasional loud "Aye?" from Mrs. Gibbons. Through the open library door Belinda saw Mrs. Bailey with two other residents discussing their respective books. The Manor was alive.

I wish Aunt Virgie could see this, Belinda thought to herself. *I think she would enjoy all of the—the commotion.*

Belinda was about to turn to the stairs when the doorbell rang. She looked about for Windsor, but since he was not nearby, Belinda went to the door herself. Foolishly, she hoped it might be Drew coming to wish her a Merry Christmas Eve. Her heart beat a bit faster as she opened the door.

A tall woman stood there, her coat wrapped tightly about her sturdy body, her hat being held in position against the winter wind.

"Oh, do come in, please," Belinda quickly invited, wondering what errand the woman had.

She moved inside, shook the snow from her clothing and turned to Belinda.

"I am not expected," she apologized, "but if it's possible I would like to see Miss Davis."

"I'm Miss Davis," Belinda responded. "Please come in."

Belinda cast a look about her. There was really no private place to take a caller. The library and the music room were occupied, and the north parlor was more than occupied. She hesitated and then motioned toward the formal parlor. She believed that it was available—at the moment.

The woman just stood and looked at her. "But I was—I was told that Miss Davis is the mistress here."

Belinda looked down at the dusty apron that covered her simple frock. She didn't look much like the mistress of such a fine Manor.

"I'm sorry—I've been preparing for Christmas," she explained with a smile. "The boxes I was digging into were dusty."

She removed the apron and tossed it on the hall table.

"Now—Miss—Miss—?"

"Tupper," supplied the woman. "Mrs. Tupper."

"Mrs. Tupper," Belinda went on, "how may I help you? Do

you have a family member staying with us?"

"Oh, no," the woman quickly replied. "I've no connections here."

Belinda waited.

"But I was told that you need a nurse," the woman said.

"Yes, we do," Belinda replied quickly.

"I—I am a nurse, miss," the woman explained. "I—I have all of my letters of reference right here," and she began to fumble in her handbag. "I—I must apologize for coming in unannounced—and on Christmas Eve. But, you see, it was really my only opportunity. If I don't get the job I—I need to take the train back home tomorrow."

"Home?" queried Belinda.

"Well—it's not really home—anymore. But we used to live in Trellis, my husband and I. He's—he's gone now. We had him here in the hospital in Boston, but even with the best care we could give him he—" She stopped herself a moment, then quickly changed the direction. "So when I heard you needed a nurse, well, I thought I'd inquire. It's foolish, I know," she admitted, tears in her eyes, "but I hate to go home—alone. I'd like to stay on—here in the city—to be near his—his resting place—at least for a while."

"I understand," said Belinda, her heart going out to the woman. She moved toward the hallway door.

"Please," she invited, "take off your coat and join the others in the parlor before the fire. They are just preparing for tea. It being Christmas Eve, Cook has prepared something special." Belinda smiled warmly and led the way toward the cozy chatter from the north parlor.

Belinda introduced Mrs. Tupper to the residents in the room and saw that she was part of the group before leaving with the references in hand. She settled herself in her room with a cup of tea and carefully read the pages. The woman was well qualified for what was needed at the Manor. Belinda smiled to herself. The last detail was in place. She would welcome the widow to the household and inform her that she had the job. *We have our nurse. And just in time, too!* Tomorrow would be Christmas.

Belinda decided to put the woman in the small bedroom at

the end of the hall until she herself could vacate the larger rooms. As soon as Christmas was over, she must lose no time in getting her things sorted and packed.

A new thought sobered Belinda. *There's really no need for me to stay on in Boston now. No need at all.*

Chapter 22

Christmas

Even before Belinda opened her eyes on Christmas morning, she could hear stirring in the house. *What is it?* she asked herself. *Why is everyone up so early? Is something wrong?*

Belinda wrapped a warm robe around her and went to investigate.

But the stirring was only the new family members rushing excitedly about. Belinda blinked in astonishment.

"It's Christmas!" shouted Mrs. Gibbons with glee.

"They are worse than children," Belinda murmured to herself and then smiled indulgently. It was nice to have them so excited about Christmas. She could well imagine that for some of them this would be perhaps the first Christmas day that had brought pleasure for many years.

Well, there's little use going back to bed now, Belinda reasoned, so she pulled back her drapes and looked out upon the new morning, clear and crisp.

The sun had not yet risen, but the wind had quieted during the night and a blanket of newly fallen snow covered everything. Trees lifted frosty branches like long silver fingers pointing toward the sky.

It will be a pretty morning when the sun comes up, Belinda sighed and caught a glimpse of a silver moon just disappearing on the western horizon.

Christmas Day. I'd hoped to be home for Christmas Day.

187

Belinda's thoughts turned, as always, to her own family and Christmases past.

We'll need both big sleighs this morning to get everyone to church, Belinda's practical side took over. *That'll be so much better than Windsor needing to make two trips.*

Potter of course did not insist that everyone attend the morning service, but she had given them the opportunity. To Belinda's delight, all ten residents had decided to participate. Windsor would drive the sleigh that he had been driving for many years, and Sid would drive the newly purchased one. Even with the two large sleighs in service, there would be no extra room.

At least we shouldn't be cold, Belinda smiled to herself. *Packed in together as we will be.*

Belinda's presence was not required at the breakfast table. Ella brought a tray to her and she lingered over it, enjoying the fruit and scones that Cook had prepared. It was Belinda's favorite breakfast, and Cook knew that. Belinda poured another cup of coffee for herself and watched the sun slowly climb into the sky, making the frosted trees glow a satiny pink.

It's a lovely day even if it's cold, Belinda observed. *I'm going to enjoy the drive to church this morning.*

Belinda was looking forward to this trip for more than one reason. Drew was to join her there. Then he would return with her for an afternoon of family games and fun followed by Christmas dinner. It promised to be a good day.

Everyone seemed in the best of spirits as each helped the other into the sleighs. Even the quiet Mr. Lewis could not keep a smile from flickering across his face now and then. Belinda was pleased to see him responding to the spirit of the morning.

Behind Belinda in the lead sleigh came Sid in the second one. Belinda waved to him and received a cheery wave in response.

Sid was settling in well to life at the Manor. He had enrolled in classes at nearby Boston University and spent most of his time poring over his books. The rest of the time he cheerfully pitched in with whatever needed doing about the house and grounds. There seemed to be no end of ways Sid found to give assistance. Both Windsor and Thomas told Belinda they enjoyed the help and company of the young man. And Ella tittered and primped everytime Sid appeared. Belinda could not fault Ella. Sid was an attractive young man and one with courtesy and understanding. And Belinda felt sure that with his ambition and discipline, Sid would do what he set out to do. He was much like his older brother. Belinda smiled.

The church service was full of worship and praise, and Belinda felt her whole heart and soul respond. Drew had taken his place between Belinda and Mrs. Simpson and clearly enjoyed the service as well. Pride glowed in the eyes of the older woman as she sat between her two grown sons. Things had worked out, after all. She was sincerely thankful as she participated in the Christmas carols.

"How did you all fit?" Drew asked Belinda as they left the church and prepared to reboard the sleighs for the ride home.

"It was quite merry, actually," Belinda laughed. "Much like the sleigh rides we used to enjoy when I was a schoolgirl back home."

Drew smiled and offered his arm to help her in. "Well, I do hope that no one tries to shove straw down my neck," he said humorously.

"Then don't sit too near Mr. Rudgers," Belinda warned. "He might try—that is, if he had some straw."

"Oh, you have a prankster in the crowd?"

"I have a notion he might try just about anything," Belinda agreed. "Although to this point he's spent most of his energy teasing poor Miss Mitton."

"And how does poor Miss Mitton respond?" asked Drew.

"Well," chuckled Belinda, "at first I don't think she was too sure just what to do. She would frown and squirm and try to stay out of his way. I think she felt that teasing was below her dignity. But then she started to warm up to it. The fact is, I think she is enjoying it tremendously. I would expect that it has been a while since a gentleman paid her that much attention."

"Ah, the weaker sex!" said Drew with an exaggerated sigh. "How subtle they are!"

They all managed to squeeze back into the sleighs and then they were off, the horses blowing and snorting, tossing their heads and wanting to run. Mr. Rudgers waved his arm in the air excitedly and called out, "Turn 'em lose, Windsor!" to which Miss Mitton shrieked like a schoolgirl. Belinda gave Drew a quick glance and caught his wink. The whole atmosphere was like one of children out for a romp, with laughter and teasing and a great deal of good-natured chatter. Belinda wondered if the sleigh load behind them was having as much fun.

They returned to the Manor with rosy cheeks, stamping their feet and looking forward to hot tea.

"That was a wonderful service," said Mrs. Bailey. "Been a long time since I've been to one as good."

"Wonder where they got that minister," said the straightforward Mrs. Gibbons. "Wonder what happened in his past to take the smile from his face. He was so serious about everything he said. Miss! Miss!" she called, trying to get Belinda's attention. "What happened to that there minister?"

Belinda shook her head. "I have no idea if anything happened to him," she responded.

"Aye?" yelled Mrs. Gibbons. "I didn't catch that."

Belinda was unable to answer again. The commotion in the hall was far too great.

Mr. Rudgers was surreptitiously holding one end of Miss Mitton's scarf, and as she tried to remove it, it refused to be dislodged. Even Mr. Lewis chuckled at the bewildered look on the spinster lady's face.

The clamor finally subsided and the residents were ushered into the north parlor for afternoon tea. Dinner was to be served at five.

Belinda watched as they settled themselves about the room in little clusters, already having formed friendships. It was nice to see them feeling at home.

"Come with me," Belinda said to Drew, and led the way to the staff room off the kitchen.

"So you've been relegated to 'staff'?" he teased her.

"And I don't mind one bit," Belinda responded merrily. "You have no idea the number of times I've envied them this coziness.

Here they sat chatting and laughing, and I sat all alone in that big dining room wishing I had some good company."

"And to you, good company is—?" prompted Drew.

"A friend," answered Belinda. "Any color, size, rank or station."

Drew nodded, knowing it was true. Belinda could never be branded as a snob.

"I'll get us some tea," Belinda said. "Just pull up a chair to the fireplace."

It was a cozy room. The staff spent many hours there. Across one end, just inside the kitchen door, was the big, sprawling table where they ate their meals. At the other end of the room several chairs were grouped around a large stone fireplace. Today a fire burned cheerily. The room, far more than a gathering place, was a workroom as well. Mending was done here. A large mangle iron was pushed up against one wall, and beside it, on the workdays of the week, the clean laundry was folded and sorted on a long, narrow table.

"If walls could talk," Drew said mostly to himself, looking about him. "I'm sure this room has buzzed from time to time as people have worked together here."

"That's an interesting thought," Belinda commented as she went for a tray of tea and biscuits.

"Cook says that's all we get," she laughed when she returned with it. "She's afraid we will spoil our appetites for her feast at dinner."

Drew looked over at the prepared table at the other end of the room. "If it tastes as good as that table looks," he told her, "I would hate to do that."

"Did I tell you the good news?" Belinda said as she poured the tea. "We have a nurse."

"Really? How did you find her?"

"Well, actually, she found us," and Belinda told Drew of the arrival of the woman the night before.

"So everything is about settled then?"

"That was the last detail to be worked out. I had so hoped to have everything in place by Christmas. And here it is. All

set. I can hardly believe it." Belinda shook her head, tears close
to the surface.

Drew was silent for several minutes as he sipped his tea.
He watched Belinda carefully. She felt his eyes upon her and
turned to meet his gaze.

"You know, you are really something," he said quietly. "Who
else but you would take this—this beautiful inheritance and—
and share it with a whole houseful of other people? You amaze
me, Belinda. You are the most unselfish person I've ever met."

Belinda's eyes fell before the open admiration in Drew's.

"Please," she said in embarrassment, "don't make a saint of
me."

"I mean it," he responded softly. "I admire you—tremendously."

"I—I'm sure that Aunt Virgie expected me to—to *use* the
house—not just harbor it," Belinda explained haltingly.

"But that was because your Aunt Virgie knew Belinda
Davis," he insisted.

Belinda shrugged slightly and took another sip of tea.

"That's what I love about your family," Drew went on.
"That's the way you all think—as though life were—were
meant to be shared with others. Unselfishness is as—as natural
as breathing."

Belinda thought about his words. Perhaps—perhaps that
was true of her father—her mother—even Luke. She had seen
it often, had taken it for granted.

"That was what convinced me there was really something
sound about Christianity," Drew continued. "I saw faith lived
and breathed in the form of your father."

Belinda's eyes were now filled with tears, thinking of her
family—her parents—on Christmas Day. She blinked away the
tears.

"I have been blessed," she said softly. "I know that. I remind
myself of it often—but"—she smiled through her tears—"it's
awfully nice to hear someone else say such kind things about
your folks."

There was a movement at the door and Ella entered.

"Windsor and Sid are on their way from the stable," she said excitedly. "Shall I bring in their tea, miss?"

Belinda nodded. "And, Ella, let Mrs. Simpson know so she can join us."

They all gathered about the open fire. The intimacy of the moment was gone for Belinda and Drew, but the chatter and laughter continued. Belinda watched Drew and Sid as they bantered back and forth and recognized the joy and pride on the face of their mother. *I'm so glad that I invited them here,* she thought to herself. *It has brought Drew so much happiness.*

But even as Belinda thought it, she also realized that she had brought to Boston the only reason likely to draw Drew back to their small hometown. His family.

The rest of the day was wonderful. Belinda wandered through the house listening to the small talk and laughter as residents played checkers or chess and enjoyed the music that wafted from the music room. Mr. Lewis surprised everyone when he drew a violin from a worn case and began to play the familiar Christmas carols along with Miss Mitton. He was a bit rusty, his fingers arthritic, and his notes not as clear as they once must have been, but the audience was appreciative and responded with applause at the end of each piece. Belinda could well imagine that the old man and his violin had both found a home.

And then it was time for Cook's Christmas dinner—the guests served in the big dining room and the staff in the staff quarters. Belinda was sure the folks who were gathered around the magnificent table in the formal dining room could not have enjoyed the meal any more than the ones in the simple, cozy staff room.

She wondered if there was just a bit of a strain at first as Windsor, Potter or Cook would look up to see her calmly sitting among them, but the feeling quickly disappeared as the laughter around the table increased. To Belinda's surprise, she discovered a genuine sense of humor in the dignified Windsor.

After dinner they all gathered together in the main parlor and sang some carols. Miss Mitton was disappointed that she couldn't accompany them on the piano, but there was no way to bring the instrument into the parlor.

Belinda asked Drew to read the Christmas story, and he did so with such feeling that many in the little congregation had misty eyes.

Sid led the little gathering in a short prayer and then eyes and thoughts turned to the gifts beneath the tree. Belinda was glad she had managed to find a last-minute gift suitable for the new resident nurse. Belinda asked Ella to do the distributing and Ella slyly asked for Sid's assistance.

There were hoots and cries of glee around the circle as each present was opened. *It's turned out to be a truly happy party,* Belinda told herself joyfully. Then it was time for the staff to go back to wash dishes and do the necessary household chores. The Manor residents returned to their fires.

Drew turned to Belinda. "This has been the most wonderful Christmas I ever remember," he told her sincerely. "Thank you for letting me be part of it."

Belinda smiled.

"Now I should be getting back. You must be very tired."

"Sid will drive you. He has already asked about it," Belinda informed him.

"I—I was hoping for a little chance to talk," Drew admitted, looking disappointed.

Belinda's eyes opened wide. "Of course," she responded, her heart all aflutter. "I'll get my wraps."

"You don't mind?"

Belinda shook her head firmly. If there was one thing she was sure of, it was that she didn't mind having a chance for a talk with Drew.

Chapter 23

Farewell

Belinda's heart was thumping wildly in her chest as Drew helped her into the sleigh. It was a beautiful night for a sleigh ride. The air was crisp and the stars overhead were bright. *Will this be a perfect end to an already perfect day?* she wondered. Sid took his seat up front and lifted the reins. "Okay, big brother," he joked, "is it to the scenic route?"

Drew laughed and told Sidney to pay attention to his driving. Sid waved a hand good-naturedly and clucked to the team.

The snow crackled beneath the runners as they moved off. Belinda felt like a young girl again, off for an evening of fun and adventure. In fact, Belinda felt about as young and light-hearted as she ever remembered.

Drew tucked the blanket closely about her and asked solicitously if she was warm enough.

Belinda wasn't sure if she would have known if she was freezing, but she nodded that she was fine.

"I really enjoyed today," Drew said again. "It was the kind of Christmas one dreams of."

"It was fun, wasn't it?" Belinda agreed.

"Did you see the faces around the Christmas tree?" Drew asked. "They were like children."

"I suppose this was the first real Christmas for many of them in years," Belinda said solemnly. "Some have come from pretty desperate circumstances. Lonely situations."

"It was hard to remember that today—watching them."

Belinda thought again about the day. It had been good—*perfect,* she decided.

"I have just one regret," she said wistfully.

"A regret?" Drew placed his arm companionably about her shoulders and pulled her closer.

"The nurse. Mrs. Tupper. I wish I would have offered to take her to—to her husband's grave. She is still so lonely. I think if I were in her situation—"

"You didn't know?" asked Drew.

Belinda shifted to look at him in the moonlight.

"Windsor took her to the cemetery," said Drew.

"Windsor?"

Drew nodded.

"How do you know?" asked Belinda.

"Sid told me. He offered to do the driving, but Windsor insisted that the drive would do him good."

"Where was I?" asked Belinda.

"You were busy—making all your new family feel at home. It was about three-thirty."

Belinda was speechless for a moment. "Dear old Windsor," she murmured at last. "The more I know of him, the more I love and respect him."

"He is rather special, isn't he?" admitted Drew.

The city streets were quiet, but now and then they passed a house where merrymaking was still in progress. Belinda laughed as they drove by one such house where the music and laughter poured out into the street.

"I guess some people like to make the celebration last just as long as possible," she commented.

Drew's arm tightened about her shoulders. She heard him take a deep breath and her heart beat more quickly. "Belinda," he began, "there's something I need to talk to you about."

Belinda felt that she might explode with the intensity of the moment. She didn't trust herself to reply so she simply nodded.

"You remember when we were kids—back home?"

Belinda nodded again.

"You remember how I shot that rabbit and spooked your horse?"

Another nod.

"Well—I—think I fell in love with you that day."

Belinda could not even nod. She had dreamed so often of hearing Drew say those words.

"And then when I discovered that it was your brother who had removed my arm," Drew went on, "I was shattered. I was so angry about losing it that I couldn't accept you. You were—were a part of it."

Belinda felt his grip tighten on her shoulder.

"And then, thanks to your pa, and God, I finally got that all straightened out."

Belinda released her breath and drew in again from the frosted air.

"And then one day I—I had the nerve—the audacity," and there was a bit of a chuckle in his voice, "to kiss you."

Belinda could feel her face flushing and was glad for the semidarkness.

"I meant that kiss—with all my heart—but—well, I knew I had no business, no business at all, expecting a girl like you to feel anything for me. Still, I couldn't help the way I felt. I wanted to see you—to come calling. In fact, I did a number of times, but each time I only got as far as your spring and then common sense would take over and I'd go home again."

"I never knew that," Belinda said in a whispery voice.

"I knew I had to go away and become an attorney before—before I ever had any right to try to win you," Drew went on. Belinda shivered from excitement rather than the cold.

"I wanted so badly to come and tell you goodbye—to ask you to have faith in me—and to wait, but I knew I couldn't expect that from you."

"Oh, but I—" began Belinda with a little gasp, but then bit her lip to keep silent.

Drew continued. "Well, I thought I was dreaming that day I met you in the law office. Here I was, an attorney now, and here you were—in the same city. It seemed like an answer to all my prayers. I couldn't believe that you had not married.

There must have been dozens of young men who would have given an arm to have you." Drew stopped, then laughed at his choice of expressions.

I was waiting for you! Belinda's heart cried, though she made no comment. *I know that now—but I didn't know it then.*

"I guess—I guess I don't have to tell you that—I still love you," Drew said softly. "I suppose I always will. I had hoped, with all my heart, that this time—that this time I would have been free to—to ask for your love in return. But as I've watched you—day after day—I've realized—" Drew's voice fell and his arm tightened again. "I know now that I can't ask that of you. If things had been different—" He let the words hang in the air.

Belinda felt something go cold within her. *No! No!* her heart protested. *Don't say that. Don't!* She wanted to throw her arms around Drew and sob against him. But she held herself upright, rigid, and forced herself to listen to what he had to say.

His voice was low, choked. She could tell that the words were as difficult for him to say as for her to hear. "I love you, Belinda, and as—as I can't—can't ask, I realized as I watched you today that I—I just can't go on as we have been—as friends. It hurts too much to see you—to keep dreaming. I think it would be better for you—for both of us—if we don't see each other anymore. You need to—to get on with your life—and I won't stand in your way."

They were almost to Drew's tenement building. Belinda was sure she would never make it. She bit her lip and choked back the tears. Drew was saying goodbye, she tried to tell herself. *Is it—is it because he's heard I'm going home and won't ask me to stay on in Boston? Doesn't he know—doesn't he realize that a girl will sometimes gladly change her mind?*

Belinda was on the verge of telling him that he had no right to judge what was best for her, but she checked her impulsiveness. There might be something else—something entirely different, something he had not said. She would not put Drew in the impossible position of asking for his explanation. He had said that their lives should go separate ways. She must accept that.

"I think far too highly of you to be anything but open and honest," Drew was saying. "I do hope you understand why—why I can't bear the thought of just being friends."

Belinda managed a silent nod. She didn't really want friendship either.

Sid cried out a loud "Whooa" to the team. Drew pulled Belinda close and tilted her face in the moonlight. "Goodbye, Belinda," he whispered and kissed her once again. Belinda could see the tears in his eyes. Then he was gone, and Sid was calling a goodnight to his older brother and moving the team forward again.

Belinda pulled the blankets closely about her, but she could not stop her shivering. She fought to remain calm, though her heart still pounded and her head whirled.

"Beautiful night for a drive," Sid called back. Belinda had no answer. She didn't trust her voice. Sid began to whistle, and Belinda pulled the blanket up around her ears to shut out the sound.

Somehow she made it home. She even managed a good night to all of those still lingering about the parlor. Then she pronounced it a very long day, excused herself, and headed for her room.

She did not even properly prepare herself for bed, but threw herself down on the ornate spread, and for the first time since she had been a small child, Belinda cried herself to sleep.

The die had been cast. There was little that Belinda could do about it, she reasoned. She arose the next morning, washed her swollen face, and began the job of sorting through her belongings.

She was going home as planned. There was nothing to hold her any longer in Boston.

All morning she sorted and packed. She tossed aside all her fancy satins and silks as they were much too ornate for her hometown. Then she eyed them again and thought of Abbie and Kate. With a bit of remodeling they could make quite suitable gowns out of the dresses. The material was lovely. She changed her mind and packed all but the two fanciest. These

she would turn over to Potter. The older woman had a knack
with a needle. She could do with them whatever she wished.

There was a rap on Belinda's door, and Ella entered. "No
one had seen you about, miss. We feared you might have taken
ill or something."

Belinda assured her that she had not. "I've been busy," she
informed Ella. "I have so much to do."

The maid looked about the cluttered room and her face fell.
"You haven't changed your mind?"

Belinda shook her head.

"I was hoping that you would, miss."

"There's no reason for me to change it," Belinda said, and
the words took more effort than Ella would ever know.

"It will just be so—so different without you here," Ella went
on frankly. "The whole staff had been hopin' that you'd stay
on."

Belinda looked up from her packing, wondering if Ella had
exaggerated—still it was nice to hear.

"Things are all arranged now," she reminded Ella. "There
is no need for me to stay around," she reiterated.

"Well, 'need' is what, miss?" asked Ella frankly. "Maybe the
clothes will be washed and the rooms cleaned, but that doesn't
mean that you aren't needed. You make this place seem—more
like a home—to all of us."

Belinda swallowed the lump that threatened to choke her.
"That is a very kind thing to say, Ella," she said softly, and
when she lifted her head to look at the girl, she saw tears in
Ella's eyes.

"I'll miss you, Ella," she said honestly.

Ella blinked away her tears and backed toward the door.
"I'll get you a tray, miss," she managed and then was gone.

The day did not get easier for Belinda. The news of her
resolve seemed to spread throughout the house and bring a
feeling of gloom. It was a compliment of sorts, but Belinda
feared the new living arrangement could not tolerate such an
atmosphere. She gave up her packing momentarily and went
down to try to stir up some merriment.

But Belinda was of no mind to stay on any longer than was

absolutely necessary. As the days slipped by, she quietly continued her preparations. She planned to be on her way by the end of the week.

When the day of her planned departure arrived, Belinda drew Windsor aside. "Windsor, I should like to be driven to the station this afternoon," she informed him quietly.

The man's eyes grew big with question. "You still plan to go?" he asked hoarsely.

Belinda nodded. "The train leaves at two," she said matter-of-factly.

"We haven't even had a proper goodbye," the butler said in a tight voice.

"Now, Windsor, what is a proper goodbye? We will say one at the door, when I'm leaving."

"That hardly seems adequate, miss," Windsor dared to contradict her.

"Well, any other kind would just be too painful," Belinda admitted and Windsor nodded his head.

"It will be painful regardless, M'lady," he told her.

Belinda fled back upstairs to do the last-minute preparations.

When the last item had been tucked away, she drew a heavy coat about her and let herself out the back door. She followed the garden paths between what had been Thomas's showy flower beds such a short time ago. Here and there a dry-looking stick acknowledged that something had lived in those beds. The snow covered all else. She was sure she would find the old gardener and his dog in the greenhouse.

"Thomas," she called as she entered the sanctuary. "Thomas, are you here?"

"Over heah, miss," Thomas's rusty voice answered and McIntyre came ambling from that direction to greet her.

"'Tis a mite chilly to be out wanderin'," Thomas observed and Belinda nodded in agreement.

"It's colder than I realized," she admitted.

"You'll be catchin' your death of cold," the old gentleman worried, looking at Belinda's feet for the warm footwear she should have been wearing.

"I'm going right back in," she informed him.

She let a moment of silence pass and then spoke again. "I came to say goodbye."

The old man's head jerked up from the tender shoot he was grafting on a rose bush. He said nothing but his eyes quizzed her.

"I'm returning home—as planned," she continued. "Everything is arranged here now."

The old man still said nothing. He laid aside his twig and his tools and looked at Belinda.

"You're shuah?" he asked at length.

Belinda nodded, tears in her eyes. This was not going to be as easy as she had hoped.

"You don't plan on being back?"

Belinda shook her head.

"We'll miss you," he said simply and turned away. It was not fast enough for him to hide the tears in his own eyes. There was silence for a moment. Thomas broke it.

"I have something foah you," he said and led Belinda to a table at the end of the greenhouse.

Curious, Belinda followed. Thomas reached for a small container, and Belinda could see a plant protruding from the soil. He handed the pot to her.

"Mind it doesn't freeze," he cautioned.

Belinda accepted the gift, unaware of what it was she held.

"It's a Princess Belinda," he said softly.

"Your rose," whispered Belinda, and more tears came to her eyes. "Thank you, Thomas."

He nodded and reached a hand down to McIntyre's head. "We'll miss you," he said again.

"And I will miss you—so much," responded Belinda. Thomas nodded. He seemed in a hurry to get the awkward goodbye over.

"Thomas," Belinda said on impulse. The old man lifted his head and blinked watery eyes.

"Would you mind—could I give you one quick hug?"

He moved clumsily to embrace Belinda. He held her much longer than she had anticipated and then they bid a quick fare-

well. Clutching her precious rose inside her coat, Belinda fled
to the big house.

The other goodbyes were no easier. She longed to just turn
and flee from the house, but she knew she couldn't. She probably would never see these people again. She would miss them
all so much. Especially the dear staff. They had been like a
family for such a long time. It was difficult to think of life
without them.

After Belinda said a hasty farewell to each of the new residents, she turned to the members of the staff. Potter blew her
nose loudly on her pocket hankie, Cook let the tears run down
her cheeks and then whisked them away with her apron, and
Ella openly sobbed. Belinda felt she couldn't endure another
minute of the emotional leave-taking. She lingered an extra
moment to whisper to Mrs. Simpson, "I'm so glad you agreed
to come." Then she gave Sid a hug and hurried out to the sleigh
after Windsor.

She continued to blow and sniff all the way to the station.
And then she still had to say goodbye to Windsor. "I have no
words to tell you how much I've appreciated you," Belinda told
the stiff butler, holding out her hand to him. He only nodded
as he solemnly shook her hand.

"You've been so kind," Belinda went on.

"I've only done my duty, M'lady," he said with difficulty, "but
you served when the duty wasn't even yours."

Belinda was puzzled at his statement.

"I saw the love you gave to Madam," Windsor said frankly.
"A love that went far beyond duty—and I loved you for it."

Belinda was touched. "You see, M'lady," and Windsor leaned
forward slightly in a confidential way, "I've never told this to a
living soul before, but—I loved her, too. Always!"

Belinda reached up on her tiptoes and placed a quick kiss
on the weathered cheek; then she turned and ran toward the
waiting train.

How beautiful, she thought as she ran, *how beautiful—and
how sad. He loved her—all these years, and he would have died
before he let her know. And just because—because he saw them*

as being from different stations in life.

Belinda climbed aboard the train with the help of the conductor and settled herself for a good weep.

Men can be so foolish! she cried in desperation.

Chapter 24

Settling In

The long train ride gave Belinda an opportunity to get herself under control. She needed every minute of it, she told herself. She was an emotional wreck. But as the miles ticked slowly by, she began to put things into better perspective.

Being back in her old hometown would be good, she assured herself—back again with her family. There would be many adjustments to be made, she was wise enough to realize, but she was capable of adjustments. She hoped that Luke and Jackson would still need a nurse. Nursing was the only vocation she had. There was no other way that she would be able to support herself—and she certainly did not plan to go crawling home again and be dependent on her ma and pa.

Belinda gently fingered the soft green petals of the rosebush she had carefully sheltered from the cold. Thomas had promised that it would be fine in the little pot until spring came again. Belinda intended to nurture it carefully.

When the train did finally pull into the local station, Belinda climbed down the steps to the familiar platform. There was no one to meet her, for she had informed no one she was to be on that particular train. She made arrangements for her luggage to be held in storage until she could get someone to pick it up.

After setting her rose bush securely in the warmth of the station, she set off for Luke and Abbie's. It was midwinter but

Belinda was hardy. Still, she was thoroughly chilled by the time she rapped on Abbie's back door.

"Belinda!" Abbie squealed and threw herself at her sister-in-law.

Belinda returned the embrace. Ruthie came running to see what the fuss was about.

"Well, look at you!" Belinda exclaimed with a hug for her niece. "My how you've grown."

Ruthie, well pleased with herself, stretched up on her tiptoes to emphasize the fact of her rapid growth.

"Come in, come in," urged Abbie. "Take off your things. How did you get here? I didn't hear a team." Her words came nonstop.

"Well, I didn't get a ride," she said. "I left my things at the station and walked."

"You walked? In this cold? Oh, Belinda. We'd no idea you'd be coming in or we'd have—"

"I know," Belinda quickly replied. "It was my own doing. I didn't warn you."

"Well, we've been hoping each day for a letter," Abbie rushed on. "The boys have hardly been able to stand it. Every day they come home from school and ask if you've sent your arrival date."

Belinda smiled. She intended to make friends with her young nephews again.

"How are they?" she asked.

"Fine. Fine," Abbie assured her, but Belinda detected a flickering of shadow in her eyes.

"How are the folks?" Belinda asked simply.

"Ma is a bit poorly," Abbie admitted before Belinda could inquire further. "Nothing serious, we hope, but Luke has put her to bed. He's out there now—just checking."

Belinda felt her body grow numb. She was unable even to voice her concern.

"The flu, Luke thinks," Abbie rushed on. "But it has really taken the starch outta her. It's been a bit hard for Pa."

"Why didn't someone let me know?" Belinda questioned.

"You didn't get Luke's letter? No, I suppose not. It is likely still on its way. Ma just took sick last Wednesday."

Belinda wanted to get home immediately. She was needed to nurse her mother.

"Is there someone who could drive me out?" she asked Abbie.

"I suppose we could get one of the fellas from the stables— but Luke should be home any minute now. He'll take you."

"I'd really like to get there as quickly as I can," Belinda urged and Abbie nodded.

"Of course," she said. "I understand. I wish the boys were home. We could send one of them over to fetch a team. Well, sit down and have a cup of tea to warm yourself up."

"I think I'll just walk over and hire a team," Belinda said, drawing her gloves back on again.

"Oh, I hate to have you do that," moaned Abbie, wringing her hands. "I know you're anxious, but it's so cold."

"It's really not that bad," Belinda tried to assure her. "Don't worry about me," and she gave Ruthie a hug, kissed Abbie on the cheek and hurried back toward town and the stables.

She was able to find a young lad to drive her out to the farm. They swung by the station, and her suitcases and trunks were loaded. The rose bush was left behind with the station agent's wife who promised to care for it until some warmer day. Then they were on their way.

Belinda knew it was her anxiety that was making her impatient, but it was all she could do to keep from shouting at the team to hurry. When at last they did pull into the yard, Luke's team was still tethered out front. Belinda was both relieved and frightened. *What is keeping Luke here so long?* she wondered.

She rushed into the house without rapping on the door, and Clark and Luke both looked up when they heard her. They were seated at the kitchen table drinking coffee.

"Belinda!" Clark cried. "Where did you come from?"

Belinda was unable to answer. She was being engulfed in a big bear hug.

"I have a driver to pay and luggage to get upstairs," she said quickly as she was passed to her brother for another big hug. "Where's Ma?"

"Up in her room—and she will be so glad to see you. I think she's sleeping right now," Luke answered.

Clark was drawing on his heavy coat to go take care of the driver and the luggage. Belinda started for the stairs as Luke too slipped into his heavy coat.

Belinda tiptoed up the stairs and quietly opened her mother's door. Marty was sleeping. Her face was pale, but she did not look seriously ill as Belinda had feared she might.

She crossed to the bed and gently laid a hand on Marty's brow; she did not feel feverish. Belinda sighed deeply in relief. Luke had cared for her well. Belinda bent to press a kiss on her mother's brow. Feeling much more at peace with the situation, she left the room. She was sure her mother needed to rest. They could talk later.

"You found her?" asked Luke as he came through the kitchen with some of Belinda's suitcases.

"She was sleeping as you said," Belinda admitted. "I decided that she might need the rest more than a chat with me."

"She will be mighty glad fer thet chat, you can bet on thet," Clark assured Belinda, laden with suitcases on his way to Belinda's old room.

Belinda removed her coat and hat and laid them on the sitting room rocker. Then she returned to the kitchen and put some wood on the kitchen fire. It was getting close to suppertime. *I hope I still know how to cook,* she joked to herself.

Clark and Luke came through the kitchen with a trunk between them. "My word, little girl," Clark said teasingly. "ya sure came home with a passel more'n ya left with."

Belinda nodded. She supposed she had.

She checked the coffeepot and was glad to find some coffee remaining. She was cold from the ride. Perhaps the coffee would help to rid her of the chill. She went to the cupboard for a cup.

Clark and Luke joined Belinda at the table. "Now catch us up on all yer news," Clark invited.

But Belinda had very little news she felt like sharing. Instead, she asked them for the news of home. She was especially anxious to hear about her mother's illness. Luke explained in detail, and Belinda nodded in understanding as he talked.

"Then she seems to have improved?" she asked when he was done with his report.

"Oh, much," he said with relief. "She was even able to take some broth today—and she kept it down, too."

Belinda felt a surge of thankfulness. "Well, I'll be here to care for her now," she said with emotion. Clark and Luke both expressed gratitude for that blessing.

Marty did continue to improve, but it was three weeks before she was totally herself again. With the assurance that her mother was completely well and could once again take over the care of the house, Belinda began to make her own plans.

"I think it's time for me to move on into town," she informed her folks after their devotions one morning.

Clark and Marty both turned to look at her.

"Luke says that Mrs. Jenkins needs nursing care. Mr. Jenkins has been having a terrible time trying to run the post office and care for her, and he hasn't been able to find any regular help."

Marty nodded. "We've heard of the Jenkins' situation," she told Belinda. "Neighbors have helped all they could, but her sickness has gone on for sech a long time."

"When do you want to go?" asked Clark.

"This morning," answered Belinda.

"I'll get the team whenever yer ready."

"Give me about half an hour," Belinda told him and left the table to get out the dishpan.

"Now, you don't need to worry none 'bout these few dishes," Marty assured her, but Belinda insisted that they do the dishes together one more time.

"Luke and Abbie will be glad to have ya back," Marty said as she placed a cup back in the cupboard.

"I've been thinking about that," Belinda said slowly. "I don't think I'm going to go to Luke's."

Marty looked surprised. "I'm sure they'll be expectin' ya," she told Belinda.

"I—I suppose they will, although I haven't said that I would be asking them for a room. But, Mama, things are different now. I'm not the young girl I was when I stayed with Luke before. I need to—to find my own way. I can't—can't make my home with Luke and Abbie forever."

Marty looked at her daughter with concern in her eyes. Belinda was speaking as though she expected that her course was set, as if she expected to always be as she was now—alone. Marty knew that the choice was Belinda's, but she did hope that her youngest would one day have a home—a real home of her own.

"Ya do what ya think best," Marty answered softly. "I'm sure thet they'll understand."

And so Belinda found herself one small room in the town boardinghouse. It was not fancy, but it was clean and the other residents were friendly. Besides, she had Luke and Abbie nearby. She could easily slip over to their house if she was feeling lonely.

She settled in as permanent day care for Mrs. Jenkins. The poor lady had arthritis so badly that she could do nothing for herself. Belinda was determined to give her the best care possible, to ease her pain as much as she could.

It wasn't the life that Belinda had dreamed for herself. But with each passing day she became more and more accustomed to it. It really wasn't so bad, and she did have her evenings to spend as she wished. She had no way to travel to the country church she had known as a girl, so she involved herself in the small-town church as Sunday-school teacher of a girls' class and secretary-treasurer for the ladies' mission group. It kept her more than busy, and the days passed by more quickly than she would have dared to think.

Tenderly she nursed her little potted rose. She was anxious for spring to make an appearance so she could set it out in her mama's flower bed. She hoped it would favor her with a bloom its first year.

Belinda did not pretend even to herself that she did not think of Boston and her friends there. She spoke of them often to her family members. But she never spoke of Drew. Her memories of him were far too painful for her to share with anyone. But each night before she retired, she would include him in her evening prayers.

Chapter 25

A Happy Ending

"I brought in your mail," Mr. Jenkins said to Belinda as he came from the front room of the building that served as the town post office. It was midday and time for his noon meal.

Belinda thanked him and reached for the two envelopes he handed her.

"How's Lettie today?" he asked, as he crossed the room toward the bedroom door.

"A little better, I think," responded Belinda, but he had already passed out of earshot as he went to check for himself.

He was soon back. "She's sleeping," he said thankfully, "and she does look a bit more comfortable than she has."

Belinda nodded and poured the soup in Mr. Jenkins' bowl. He sat down to hurry through his lunch before the jangling of the bell would summon him to care for another customer, and Belinda turned again to her mail.

One of the letters was from Ella. Belinda smiled as she laid it aside. She would save the enjoyment of reading it until she was alone.

The larger envelope bore the inscription of Keats, Cross and Newman, and Belinda quickly tore open the envelope.

"Oh, bother!" she exclaimed as she read the contents.

"Something wrong?" asked Mr. Jenkins.

"No, not wrong. Just a nuisance. I need to sign more papers. I thought I had already signed everything they could possibly

211

come up with—but it appears they've found more."

Mr. Jenkins merely nodded. It didn't sound like much to fuss about.

"The only problem is that they must be signed in the presence of an attorney, and that means I will have to travel—"

But Mr. Jenkins quickly cut in, "Got one here now, ya know."

"No, I didn't know," responded Belinda. "Since when?"

"Started up 'bout a week ago. Has his office over in thet little buildin' by the hardware store."

Belinda was relieved. "Well, that will work much better. I was worried about having to ask for some time off."

"You can slip over tonight," Mr. Jenkins went on. "I'll watch Lettie. Or you can run over right now—iffen ya like."

"No. Tonight will be fine. Then I can get these papers back in tomorrow's mail."

Mr. Jenkins nodded and finished his lunch. He was almost finished when the bell began to jingle.

"Drat it!" he exclaimed and took another big bite of his slice of bread. "Almost made 'er thet time," and he hurried from the room to his little post office.

While Mrs. Jenkins slept, Belinda washed the dishes and tidied the three small rooms. By the time the woman awoke, Belinda was ready to devote her full attention to her patient. She made her as comfortable as she could and settled herself in a chair by the bed to read to the woman. Mrs. Jenkins seemed to rest much easier if her mind was busy listening to a story.

Mr. Jenkins remembered his promise and appeared at the door around five o'clock. "I believe thet law office closes at five-thirty," he said to Belinda. "You'd best run on if ya want to git thet cared fer tonight."

Belinda nodded, checked her patient once more and pulled on her coat and galoshes.

It's staying light longer, she told herself as she hurried toward the hardware store. *That must mean spring is somewhere on the way.* It was a pleasant thought.

She found the small building just as Mr. Jenkins had described it. Above the door was a simple sign, "Law Office," and on the door itself the invitation, "Please walk in." Belinda did so.

The room was simply furnished with a large desk, three straight-backed chairs, some shelves lined with large law tomes, and a large set of file drawers. His back to the door, a man bent over the drawers, probably searching for some elusive file folder.

"Come right in," he called. "Be with you in a moment."

Belinda gasped. *Surely—?* The man's head came up and she gasped again.

"Drew?"

Drew stood upright, his eyes mirroring the surprise that Belinda had felt.

"Belinda!"

"I'm—sorry," Belinda stammered. "I didn't know—" and she turned abruptly and ran back out the door.

"Belinda—wait," Drew called after her, but Belinda rushed on.

She was blinded by tears and stumbling along through the rutted snow when Drew caught up with her.

"Belinda, please, wait. What is it? Is something wrong?"

He clasped her shoulder and tried to turn her to face him, but she shook herself free and moved on. He fell into step beside her.

"Please, Belinda. Please," he begged. "We need to talk."

Belinda stopped then and lifted her face to meet his look evenly.

"We have already talked, Drew. Remember?"

He flinched as if he had been struck. "I know," he said in a quiet voice. "I know. But what are you—"

"There doesn't seem to be much else to say," Belinda cut in coldly, and shrugging off Drew's hand, she hurried toward the rooming house.

She spent a miserable evening. She still could not believe it. Here she was back home, thinking she had left Drew in Boston reunited with his mother and brother, and here he was establishing himself, it would appear, right back in their hometown. "I can't go through it again—the—the love and rejection.

I can't," sobbed Belinda aloud. She shook with the intensity of the feelings that kept sweeping through her.

Her eyes red from weeping, Belinda did not bother going down for supper. She knew that the others would look at her with curiosity and concern. She had no desire to be asked sympathetic questions.

She tried to read, but the pages blurred. She paced the floor and fidgeted by turn. The evening dragged on; then at eight o'clock there was a knock on the door. Belinda decided not to answer it, but it came again.

"Belinda," came a soft call. Belinda recognized Luke's voice. She knew she must answer or he'd be out looking for her. She let him in.

"Hello," he said in his usual jovial way; then he stepped in, walked straight to her window and stood with his back to her, looking out at the lights of the small town.

"How is your patient?" he asked after a few silent moments.

"She's—doing slightly better, I think," Belinda responded.

"Good," said Luke.

Then he continued. "I dropped by home today. Ma looks much better."

"Oh, that's good!" said Belinda. There was a pause.

"The kids want to know when you're coming over," went on Luke.

Belinda managed a smile. "Tell them I'll be over soon," she replied. "I'm looking forward to some free time on Saturday. Maybe I can make it then."

"Fine," nodded Luke.

"You been busy?" asked Belinda.

But Luke didn't bother to answer her question. He turned to look at her and said instead, "We just had a visitor."

"Oh," responded Belinda, her eyebrows raised. "Who?"

"Drew." Luke watched carefully for Belinda's reaction. It was immediate. She caught her breath in a ragged little gasp and quickly turned her back.

"Is he the reason you came home?" asked Luke.

"Of course not," denied Belinda. "Why do you ask that? I had planned for months to come home."

Luke nodded. "He seemed terribly upset," he continued.

"Why?" asked Belinda innocently.

"Well, for one thing, he had the feeling that you needed an attorney for something—but you left his office without getting whatever you needed."

"I—I was just taken completely by surprise," Belinda confessed. "I'd no idea he was back in town."

"I didn't realize that running into old friends was such a— a traumatic experience," commented Luke.

Belinda flushed. "I guess I did respond—rather—hastily," she admitted.

"I thought perhaps there was something more," Luke prompted.

"Like—?" began Belinda.

"I've no idea. Would you like to tell me?"

Belinda lowered her face and shook her head.

"But he *isn't* the reason that you came home?" Luke asked again.

"No-o," Belinda replied, then added honestly, "but he—he might be the reason I didn't stay in Boston."

"I don't understand," said her big brother.

Belinda lifted tear-filled eyes. "I didn't know that—that Drew was in Boston until last fall. It was so good to see him. I—I thought he felt that way, too. I—I even thought that he might care. Well, he maybe did—in a way. At least he said he did—but he also said that because of—the circumstances— whatever he saw them to be—that we—he wouldn't be seeing me again."

Luke nodded.

"So I came on home—as I had planned. Though I—I knew that I'd stay—if—if he asked me to. But he didn't and—I didn't expect to ever see him again—and then quite unexpectedly he—he—"

But Belinda could not go on. She turned her back again as the tears began to flow freely.

"Did you know that Drew thought you intended to stay in Boston to administrate the home you had established?" Luke asked.

Belinda shook her head, her back still to her brother.

"Did you know that it was always his intention to return here to set up practice?"

"No," she said after a long pause.

"Did you know that he very nearly laid aside his lifelong dream of helping people in his own hometown so he might be free to stay in Boston and marry you?"

Belinda's shoulders shook. "No."

"Did you know that he felt that to ask you to marry him would be denying you of all the good things you had learned to appreciate?"

"No," sobbed Belinda.

Luke moved across the room to place his hands on Belinda's trembling shoulders. "What in the world did you two talk about all that time, anyway?" he asked in a teasing voice.

"Oh, Luke," sobbed Belinda and she turned to Luke's arms and lowered her head to his shoulder.

He held her and let her weep.

"You know what I would suggest?" he said softly when the sobs had subsided. Belinda shook her head.

"I would suggest that you start over. And this time *talk*."

"Oh, Luke," cried Belinda. "I think it's too late."

"Then what's he doing here waiting right outside the door?" Luke asked with a chuckle.

"He—he's here?" Belinda gasped.

"He's here. And he'll be knocking that door down if I don't soon let him in."

"Oh, my!" cried Belinda, her hand going first to her face and then to her hair. "I must look one awful sight."

"I wouldn't expect him to notice," Luke replied gently, then gave her one more squeeze before he released her and opened the door for Drew.

"Belinda?" Drew entered the room hesitantly. "May I come in?"

Belinda silently nodded.

"I—I've really botched everything, haven't I?" he said with such a tremor in his voice that Belinda wanted to reach out to him, but she stood rooted to the spot.

"I thought you felt your work was in Boston—with the elderly—"

Belinda nodded again in understanding.

"I knew—I've always felt that I was to come back here," he went on.

Belinda managed a shaky little laugh. "Silly, wasn't it? We both thought we knew what the other was thinking when—"

But Drew had closed the distance between them. He reached his hand to her face and tipped her chin upward. "Is it too late—to start again?" he asked softly.

Belinda couldn't shake her head. He was holding her against him. She knew she'd never squeeze a word past her tight throat. She only looked at him and then she shyly put her hands on his shoulders.

"I love you," whispered Drew. "I always have. Would—will you marry me?"

Belinda looked for a long time at the man she loved. She wanted to answer. She even tried to say the word, but still she was unable to speak. Her arms slipped around his neck and he must have taken that as affirmation, for Belinda found herself being tenderly kissed.

Belinda judged it to be the most glorious spring she had ever experienced. Each day seemed brighter, cleaner, more perfect than the last. Marty just smiled at her daughter. She had watched love bloom before.

Drew found a small house on the edge of town and made arrangements to rent it. Belinda spent hours dreaming of how she would fix this and paint that and Drew proved to be handy with minor repairs.

"It's going to be just perfect," Belinda enthused. "I can hardly wait to move in."

Drew smiled. The place certainly wasn't perfect, he realized, especially after what Belinda had been used to in Boston. But Drew no longer felt worried about asking her to share his dreams. Love was too evident on her face, and he knew instinctively that they would be happy together.

One day as Belinda was tending her special potted plant, she decided she couldn't wait until they actually occupied the small cottage. Her rose needed planting. When the sun came up smilingly in the springtime sky, spilling its warm promises upon the earth, Belinda carefully lifted her potted rose and headed for the small cottage.

Gently she eased the small bush from its confining container and placed it tenderly, securely into the hole that she had dug.

"Grow, little rose," she whispered as she poured water into the hole and eased the dirt back in place. "I hope you will be happy here. As happy as I intend to be. You are to make our home beautiful on the outside—and I will try to make it beautiful on the inside."

Belinda rose to her feet, studied her soiled hands and smiled with inner joy.

"Oh, I hope you bloom," she told the rose. "I hope you'll bloom *this year*." She was silent for a moment and then continued. "But if you don't—I'll wait. I feel prepared to wait now. I— I finally feel settled—ready for life."

The wedding was set for August at the little church in the country. By then Drew's law practice was becoming comfortably established. The small cottage was reasonably refurbished and furnished, and Belinda had busied herself with hanging curtains and scattering braided rugs. Though the little house was simple, Belinda was gloriously happy. It wouldn't be long before she would be Mrs. Drew Simpson.

Mrs. Simpson and Sid came for the wedding. Drew gently chided his mother when he and Belinda met the train.

"When I asked you in Boston concerning Belinda, why didn't you tell me that she had already gone home?" he asked.

"I had me no idea what had happened between you two," Mrs. Simpson admitted. "I felt that there was something strange going on when two very dear friends suddenly didn't know each other's plans."

"So you told me that Belinda would need to speak for herself?"

Mrs. Simpson shrugged. "What else could I say? I had no

intention of intruding on Belinda's privacy."

Drew put his arm around Belinda's waist and pulled her close. "Well, I forgive you Ma—now that things have worked out," he laughed.

Belinda just smiled. Tomorrow was to be the happiest day of her life.

"Are you ready?" Clark asked his youngest daughter and Belinda smiled her answer.

"It's a shame," said Clark seriously as he bent to kiss the top of her head.

"What's a shame?" Belinda asked innocently.

"It's a shame I have run out of daughters. Each bride jest gets prettier an' prettier."

"Oh, Pa," Belinda laughed, but her cheeks were glowing.

"Happy?"

"I've never been happier. I think I'm about to burst," admitted Belinda.

"Strange," mused Clark. "After all these years—you and Drew."

"It's not strange at all," smiled Belinda dreamily. "I—I think that it's just as God always meant it to be. He—He just had to wait for me to grow up."

Epilogue

Dear Reader,

We are leaving the Davises at this point in their lives. I realize that there is much more we could say about their ongoing family—but it has really grown too large and scattered for us to comfortably keep up with all their doings.

Many have suggested a reunion to bring all of the western family back to join Marty and Clark at the home farm. It sounds like fun. But it is almost impossible. For one thing, there are now far more characters than a reader—or the writer—can properly keep straight. Secondly, such an event was unlikely in the days that we are reliving in the stories. The distance was too great and the travel too difficult and expensive for all the family to be able to make the trip.

I am not going to fill you in on the future happenings of the Davises. I am leaving that to your imagination. Perhaps you have a special way that you wish the series to end.

Thank you for traveling with me. I pray as I write each story that something that is told, or even implied, might strike some responsive chord in a heart—somewhere—and that God will speak to you in a special way. He is able to do that, I know—and that is why sharing the stories with you has been so special for me.

God bless!

Oke   1261

Oke, Janette
Love finds a home

Oke   1261

Oke, Janette
Love finds a home

Tracy Alliance Church